Beg Me

Beg Me

the STEELE BROTHERS series
book IV

JENNIFER PROBST

Dedication

To the numerous authors who write beautiful BDSM erotic stories that touch my heart and shatter my mind. Your talent humbles me. Reading your work has been a pleasure. Special thanks to:

Lexi Blake, Shayla Black, Cherise Sinclair, CD Reiss, Pepper Winters, Joey W. Hill, Stacey Kennedy for your amazing series

There are so many more but I'd need a book to list them!

Dear Readers,

I loved writing this erotic, BDSM novella, but many of my loyal readers have come to expect a sexy, humorous contemporary romance filled with cute dogs, witty banter, amazing sensual tension, and some open door, arousing sex scenes.

This book is different.

The scenes are BDSM intense and there are many of them. It isn't a light, funny type book, so please be warned. I'd hate to lose my readers by having them expecting a brand that is not represented with the Steele Brother series.

Thank you, as usual, for reading.

Chapter One

*R*EMINGTON STEELE KICKED BACK ON THE leather chaise lounge, crossed his arms in front of his chest, and stared at his brothers. Hard. Something big was brewing and he didn't like it. As the youngest in the crew, he had to be stronger, faster, and smarter than them in order to survive. And this little get-together stunk of a good old fashioned Steele Brother intervention.

"Real nice of you to welcome me to Vegas with a party," he said. "So, where are your better halves?"

They relaxed in a private VIP room at The Bank, a top-rated club housed in the Bellagio hotel. Remington loved the sleek black, gold, and mirrored elegance of the decor. The mix of jungle and hip-hop music vibrated from the speakers, and the glass encased dance floor packed with writhing bodies floated in the air, serving as the focal point. His oldest brother, Rick, lifted his beer and took a long sip. "Doing girly stuff. Like we're doing manly stuff. Just because we're hooked up doesn't mean we don't know how to party on our own."

Rem held back a laugh, especially when his other two brothers, Rome and Rafe, nodded in agreement. Oh, yeah, they were done. Blissed out from love, sex, and all that cotton candy stuff that filled a man's brain and connected straight to his dick.

The pain rippled through him, but thankfully it didn't cut right to his heart like it had a few years ago. He'd experienced love once. He'd hoped to experience it again, but Rem wasn't that lucky. Five years of looking and instead, he only found a pale imitation of his first love over and over, until he'd become so frustrated he turned into a bit of a hermit. The call from his brothers had been his lucky Ace, especially on the heels of yet another broken relationship. Vegas was a fresh start, with endless possibilities. Though he doubted he'd find what his brothers had, maybe he could at least soothe the emptiness for a while. Hot women, flashing lights, and buckets of money was a nice distraction.

"If this is a party, why do I feel like I'm being set up for something?" Rem asked, studying his siblings. Rick, who looked a bit like Thor without the cool hammer, kept his gaze averted. Rome, who was like a George Clooney look-a-like, sporting pre-mature grey hair and steely eyes that kept his lover Sloane in check, cleared his throat. Rem wished to God he'd been able to claim Thor or Clooney as his birthright instead of the ridiculous 1980's show, *Remington Steele*, which had launched Pierce Brosnan's career. His mother had been a fervent viewer and named her fourth son in honor of the smooth, charming agent. Even worse, when Rem popped out with blue eyes and black hair, his mother declared it fate. Rem had taken a terrible ribbing from both his brothers and friends' parents who had also watched the show on television.

His other brother, Rafe, took a shot of Jack Daniels and leaned forward, his palms on his knees. His buzz cut had grown in and he now sported brown curls that matched the brown of his eyes. Former military, and a newly admitted male sub to his lady love, Summer, he spoke calm and steady, like Rem was about to jump out the window.

"We're worried about you, Rem."

He arched a brow. "Funny, a few months ago these two called me because they were worried about you. Now I'm the one in emotional trouble? Trust me, dude, I haven't gone through anything close to you. I'm fine."

Rafe returned from his overseas assignment with a medal for bravery, a bit broken, and a lot lost. But since he moved to Vegas and met Summer, a new peace emanated from his frame, along with a happiness Rem had never seen before. Got him all choked up. And he adored Summer, with her sunny smile and sweet disposition. He still couldn't believe she put on a cat suit and dominated his brother at night, but damned if Rem wasn't proud of Rafe for being true to himself and finding love.

"We think *you* think you're fine," Rome cut in. "But *we* don't. You practically radiate anger and frustration. And we all know those emotions don't go well with being a Dom."

Temper flicked from his narrowed gaze. "You questioning my ability to be safe with my submissives?" he asked.

Rick groaned. "No, dude, we all know you'd never hurt anyone or lose control. That's half the problem. You're so wound up that nothing seems to satisfy you. Or more to the point: no one. I talked to Dan at Chains and he said you're having trouble finding women to play with."

Fuck. He didn't need Rick's friend tattling on him. Chains was a superior BDSM club he'd joined once he got to Vegas. He enjoyed the atmosphere and openness of public scening, but hadn't been able to connect with anyone on a deeper level. Rem didn't mind. He enjoyed teaching the newer doms and demonstrating technique, but kept himself removed from going into a full-fledged scene.

Frustration simmered. His brothers were right. Eventually, he needed to engage in a scene and wring out the anxiety and scar tissue building. "I'm still settling in," he said. The excuse sounded weak to his own ears. "I'll be fine."

"Well, we got you a present," Rome said. "And if you don't use it you'll hurt our feelings."

"Ah, shit, I don't want a stripper tonight, guys."

Rafe laughed, then handed him a card. It was black and gold with the name FANTA-C scrolled in embossed lettering. Rem flicked the card over and found a phone number. "What's this?"

His brothers shared a meaningful look that, as the baby, had always annoyed the crap out of him. "That's the exclusive matchmaking agency we all used. Call the number and tell them I referred you," Rafe said.

Rem spurted out a laugh and reached for his own beer. It was official. His brothers were certifiable. "I do not need help finding a woman," he stated. "I'm insulted you think I need an escort service."

Rome elbowed Rick. "See? They need to change the name of the place, it does sound like we're getting him a hooker."

"Listen, it's not an escort agency, I swear," Rafe said. "You call the number and fill out confidential forms that details your perfect night with your perfect woman. Anything goes. If they find a match, they call. If you don't hear from them, it's because they don't have a woman who's your perfect mate."

Rem stared. "You are crazy. Do you actually think you met your women because of the juju of an agency called FANTA-C?"

"Yes," they all said in unison.

Holy crap, they really did believe it. He stared at the card and waited. No shock. No tingle. Nothing. It was just an ordinary card with an ordinary service that had fooled his brothers. Weird. His brothers were dealers and bred to spot bullshit or a bad play a light year away. They weren't the type to believe in magic and love and white picket fences.

Were they?

Remington wondered if he was missing something. A piece of a complex puzzle revolving around this mysterious FANTA-C. Maybe he needed to try it out himself. Prove to his brothers nothing special happened and it was just pure luck that led them to their mates.

"Okay. I'll call tomorrow."

Rafe grinned. Rick and Rome looked relieved. "Oh, after you call, burn the card," Rafe said.

"WTF? Now you're scaring me."

Rick shook his head. "Seriously. It's the rules."

"Am I joining a cult? How'd you get this card if you have to burn them?"

"After your match is complete and successful, FANTA-C gives you one card for a referral. You're mine, dude. Don't blow it," Rafe said.

He let out a shout of laughter. "Fine. I'll make the call. I'm too intrigued at this point to back out."

His brothers lifted their glasses in a mock salute. "To the night of your life."

Rem clinked his shot glass to theirs and drained it in one swallow. Maybe it's exactly what he needed. He felt so damn...lost. He had everything a man could want on the surface, yet his gut burned for more.

Rem smothered the messy feelings and concentrated on his party.

Chapter Two

*C*ARA WINTERS TOOK A DEEP BREATH to calm her rapidly beating heart. Excitement and nerves swirled together in an elegant cocktail she craved to drink in one gulp. It was always like this before a meeting with a Dom. But tonight was so very different than others. Tonight, she'd experience her deepest, darkest fantasies.

Her hands shook slightly as she ran them down her barely there skirt. This dom had been precise about his expectations and requirements for the evening. A bottle of champagne was on ice—"Ace of Spades" Brut Gold to be exact, and two crystal flutes flanked the bucket. The suite was opulent and lush, set off the main strip of Vegas at a hotel that FANTA-C owned. The agency confirmed it was used often for many of their clients, completely safe, and discreet. Decorated in rich burgundy and silver, gilded mirrors, plush carpeting, and a master bed and bath in gold and Italian tile made Cara feel sinfully spoiled. She hoped to use the spa tub and steam shower.

Thank goodness the dom didn't order her to greet him in standard sub position—on her knees, naked, with legs spread. Though her friend said FANTA-C was a trusted agency, she wanted to be able to talk to the dom that she was trusting her wildest fantasy to, even though she'd sent her list of do's and don'ts to him already. If the connection wasn't there, or if she got a weird feeling in her gut, Cara was walking out the door. She'd already phoned her girlfriend with the exact location and room number. Melanie was on stand-by to rescue her if needed.

A soft knock on the door interrupted her nervous thoughts.

Cara hesitated only a moment. Then opened it.

Oh…My…God!

Remington Steele.

Her first love. Her first lover. Her first heartbreak.

The shock jolted through her like an electrical current. Her body froze, but her gaze hungrily slid over him, noting the delectable changes over the years. He was leaner. Harder. Sooty black hair spilled messily over his forehead, framing aqua blue eyes. Once, those eyes were filled with burning heat. Now, they reminded her of a chilly winter morning, flecked with shards of ice.

His features were still hard and carved from stone, from his sharp Roman nose, square jaw, and slashed cheekbones. His upper lip was thin, setting off the plump lower one that had a habit of kicking up in a half smile. He'd always dressed simply, in dark wash jeans, t-shirt, and loafers, as if he could care less what he threw on his body.

Oh, God, his body. Cara had never forgotten that body.

Whiplash strong. Lean muscles. Eight pack abs from his love of the gym. Corded arms and powerful thighs. Skin a warm, toasty brown. Cara still remembered the patterns of dark hair on his massive chest, and her fingers curled with the need to reach out and touch him.

Of course, she didn't. As her previous Dom years ago, he'd never allowed her to touch without permission. As the man she'd abandoned without explanation, Cara knew her touch was not welcome anymore.

Waves of tightly wound energy snapped around him. Underneath, Cara caught the sexual chemistry between them flare to life and crackle like a live wire. It was still there. Even after years apart, the moment they came near each other, the connection took over, drawing them together like magnets doomed to never separate.

Cara shivered. "I don't understand," she managed. Her voice came out husky. "What are you doing here?"

His gaze flicked over her. Cara knew well how Rem hid his emotions like a master, not giving anything away until he was ready. It used to cause nervousness and stress. Now, she only felt acceptance. And excitement.

"This is the room FANTA-C booked for me. I sent my specifications to them about what I wanted and they sent them to my date," he said.

"I'm your date."

Silence fell. His face tightened, and those arctic eyes grew even colder. "Did you know about this?"

Cara shook her head. Wrapped her hands around her chest, trying to hide behind the skimpy corset she wore. Disapproval radiated from his figure. He'd always hated when she tried to block her body from his view. Some things never changed. "No. I wouldn't have done that to either of us."

Misery choked her throat. How had this happened? Once, this man had held her in his arms and promised to marry her one day. Now, he was a distant stranger, looking at her with disdain and regret. Not that she blamed him. She'd run like a coward, refusing to talk to him, and shattering his heart. Cara deserved his disapproval.

She straightened to full height, which was almost six foot in her four-inch heels. She held his gaze, refusing to flinch from the emptiness she found there. "I'm sorry this happened. I...I had no idea you were in Vegas or were a client of the agency. This was a mistake. I'll call them and explain so maybe they can send you someone else."

She turned on her heel to walk away.

"Cara."

She jerked at the sound of her name from his lips. His voice deepened to the familiar dark, commanding strains of a true Dom. Her body responded instantly, her nipples growing hard and her muscles already relaxing in surrender. She fought off her response with sheer determination. "Yes?"

"There won't be any need for the call."

A frown creased her brow. "I don't understand."

"You're my match for tonight. Out of all the women, in all the damn world, they picked you. For my fantasy." Spellbound, Cara watched as he picked up a black duffel bag from the floor, shut the door behind him, and stepped into the room. Testosterone blasted her in all its delicious glory, allowing her to slip into that beautiful place of abandon, to give over to a man ready to care for her, push her, control her. How had his eyes turned from cold to pure blistering heat? Rem stopped inches away. His gaze narrowed as he slowly reached out to grasp her chin, forcing her head back. "You ran away from me once. I won't allow that again. You need a man to command you tonight. A man to take everything you have to give and push you for more, until you break, until there's nothing left you haven't surrendered. I'm the man that's going to do that, Cara. You owe me, that. Do you understand?"

She shook, helpless against his gaze, his voice, and his electrifying touch. Karma cycled around and kept her in its merciless grip. It was as if all the running and avoiding she'd done over the years came down to this moment. There was nowhere left to go. Only this man she'd once loved and left; the one man she'd never been able to forget. The one man who could make all her fantasies come true.

Cara barely managed a whisper. "Yes."

"Then let's begin."

Chapter Three

*R*EMINGTON KNEW THE EXACT MOMENT she decided to stay. The glint of acceptance in her meadow green eyes made him want to roar in satisfaction and beat his chest like an ape. Instead, he kept his control, wrapping it around him tight, and dropped his hand from her chin.

Inside, he shook like a willow tree caught in a hurricane.

She was here.

Cara Winters.

God, how had she grown more beautiful? As a young woman, she'd radiated a fresh-faced sweetness that grabbed his heart from first look. Those riotous red curls had been tamed and now curved straight and sleek against her cheeks. Her skin was still a pale, pure cream he longed to taste, with a generous portion of freckles over the bridge of her pert nose. Her Irish green eyes still stunned an onlooker, with the swirl of gold around the iris, pulling a man in and spinning him in a web of fogginess. Rem always loved the generous portions of her body, her wide hips, lush breasts, and plump lips. When she was younger, she'd always tried to hide, telling him too many times she was fat. It took time, but by doling out strict punishments for each infraction, eventually she'd stopped insulting herself, and him, by putting down her body. His hand tingled at the memory of spanking her gorgeous ass, his favorite part of her anatomy. The way she'd wiggle and scream, trying desperately to pull away though she'd grown so wet and hot he ended up fucking her before the punishment was even done.

Crap. His dick grew hard, pulsing against his jeans like he was a kid again. He'd fallen for her in his freshman year at college when they were only nineteen years old. English 101. They'd been tortured with poetry, and the instructor forced them to recite a poem aloud to the group. He never forgot the bright flame of her hair hiding her face as she ducked her head to read. The slow, seductive baritone of her voice, the trembling of her fingers as she clutched the book was a moment in time that was forever etched in his mind. He'd fallen hard right then and there. Asked her out. And fell in love with her over the next few months.

The memories crashed in his head. College sweethearts. The odds had been against them, but Remington knew she was the one he wanted. He'd already known his tendencies for dominance in the bedroom, and she was a pure hearted submissive, full of sweetness and the need to surrender to him. Cara hadn't wanted to admit she was submissive though, not liking the term or assumptions. He tried showing her all the pleasures of letting him take charge in the bedroom, and her body lit up under his instruction. Still, Rem figured they'd take it slow and explore different levels as she became more comfortable. They graduated, and he decided to go to dealer school in Atlantic City. They moved in together while she studied history and worked on her master's degree, planning to teach at the college level. Everything had been perfect. Planned out. They'd been happy. Their future bright with endless possibilities.

Until she disappeared.

Now, she stood before him. Wanting to be submissive. *His* submissive. Rem had the chance to find the truth, and experience the one thing that haunted him throughout the years.

Cara Winter's full submission.

He motioned to the velvet chaise. "Sit down and let's talk first."

Her fingers clenched, and then slowly relaxed. Her chest rose as she dragged in a breath, calming herself, and walked over to the chaise. Her motions were elegant. Simplified. She'd grown into herself and achieved full power, owning her curves and body with a pride that elicited a raw lust. Her breasts spilled over the black corset, cinching in at the waist and flaring at the hips. The black skirt barely covered her full ass, clinging to her flesh and stretching to accommodate as she strode across the room. Muscled legs flexed, working the four inch black stilettos, he'd instructed her to wear. Rem imagined her heels digging into his thighs as he fucked her. Imagined her spread-eagled against the wall, while those heels tilted her ass up like a gift made for him and only him.

Fuck. He needed to get his shit together before she realized he was acting like a horny teen rather than an experienced Dom. She couldn't know how badly he'd missed her, or how often he'd thought of her over the years. If he was to own her submission, he needed to be in full control at all times.

Rem re-focused and sat across from her. Steepling his fingers together, he waited in perfect silence, gathering his thoughts. The old Cara would've ducked her head. Fidgeted. Sighed impatiently. The new Cara looked back at him with a steady gaze, completely still, and focused on his next action. His gut twisted in arousal, warring with anger. Where had she learned such control? How many men had she given herself to after she ran from him? Had he been ƒ disappointing she needed to replace him? R tamped down on the bitterness and spoke like a bit more background before we cont⸀ received your list of hard and soft limits. ⸀ anything I need to know about that's a tr

"No," she said quietly.

He'd memorized the list so he ti⸀ items that concerned him. "

17

acceptable. You said no blood or scarring. What about marking? Bruises?"

"Marks or light bruising is fine."

"Anal is a soft limit. Have you tried it before?"

"I've never tried it but I'm curious."

"You've played with an array of toys before. What's your favorite?"

Her skin flushed a delicate pink. "Vibrator with clitoral stimulator."

"Yes, one of my favorites, too." Her flush deepened but she kept her gaze on his. Nice. "Sexual intercourse is permissible?"

"Yes."

"You want me to push your limits, Cara. Hard. I need to be sure you're ready for this. I'm a strict Dom, and I will do things to your body, to your mind, that will break you down. I will go deep, and if you fight me, I'll fight back."

Her pupils dilated, so her eyes turned more gold than green. She swallowed and twisted her fingers together. "I wouldn't expect anything less of you, Sir."

The title sang in his ears and stiffened his dick. How long had he craved her to call him Sir without prompting? The term did odd things to his heart, bringing back a tidal rush of memories he didn't want to probe. He kept his attention on the moment, to the woman she was now, and that she needed from him.

Because his fantasy had been the same exact thing.

A woman he could break. A woman he could conquer. A woman he could heal.

A woman who could heal him.

"What is your safe word?"

"Red."

"You will use yellow to slow things down. Do you have any concerns before we begin?"

"Remington?"

His name rolling from her plump lips nearly brought him to his knees. She used to whisper in his ear right before she came, as if repeating his name over and over helped her hold onto something stable. He fought to keep the emotion from his face. "You will call me Sir."

Grief flickered in her green eyes but he convinced himself it was just a trick of the light. "I'm sorry, Sir. I need to know if this—if this is okay. Should we talk about what happened?"

"We both have something the other needs. Tomorrow, we'll part and never see each other again. Tonight, you will not lie to me. You will give me everything I ask, and I will take care of you because I'm your Dom until dawn. Do you understand?"

Her lower lip trembled, and she bit down hard, as if trying to find her courage. Rem studied her. Waited. Now was the time fear struck, and the reality of their situation was total. The ghosts of the past shimmered around them, taunting. It was her decision. He only had as much control as she gave him, and she needed to be ready if the evening would be what they both craved.

Her breath shuddered from her chest. "I understand."

Rem cocked his head.

"Sir."

"Very good. Our scene will begin. Please go to the edge of the bed, remove your clothes, and greet me in sub position."

Cara rose from the chaise, walked to the edge of the king size platform bed, and began untying her corset.

Chapter Four

*T*HE SHEER INTENSITY OF THE SCENE unveiled before her and part of her wanted to scream "Red" and get the hell out of dodge.

Cara couldn't believe he wanted to stay. When she took off without warning, she told herself it was for the best. She didn't want him to believe in a future that didn't exist for them. Through the years, Cara had accepted the truth of what she had done to the man she loved. She'd brutally hurt him in order to avoid confrontation. To avoid the questions he would've asked and she wouldn't have wanted to answer.

But he was here. Tonight, she'd been given a second chance to be the submissive she dreamed of being with him. Cara refused to run again, no matter how difficult facing his pain and her choices became.

She concentrated on the automatic motions of her fingers as she unlaced the corset from the front, and shimmied out of the material. Her large breasts hung free, the cool air caressing her nipples and turning them into tight points. Cara bent to pull down her skirt, and step out of the minuscule fabric. Excitement gathered low in her belly as each item of clothing was removed, until she stood naked in front of her Dom, bared for only his pleasure.

Remington feasted on her with his gaze, touching every inch of skin as if he planned exactly what he was going to do with her. When they'd been in college, Cara had been ashamed of her body. She compared herself to magazine covers and skinny models, always finding herself lacking, wondering when he'd leave her. Rem always punished her for insulting what he said belonged to both of them. She never realized the gift he'd given her early in life, his complete and total devotion to every single part of her.

She just hadn't been ready to accept the gift.

This time, she reveled in the raw lust that twisted his lips and gleamed from his blue eyes. This time, she stood proudly in front of him, knowing he received pleasure from her full breasts and curves, her generous ass and the way she held her shoulders back.

"Should I take off the shoes, Sir?" she asked.

"You may leave them on."

The burgundy carpet was plush and thick. She dropped gracefully to her knees, widening her stance, clasping her hands behind her back to thrust out her breasts. Her head bent slightly as she dropped her gaze downward. Cara focused on the breath filling her lungs. In. Out. Calm began to seep into her, bit by bit, and her surroundings came into glorious, sharp awareness.

His scent hit her first. Pleasure tingled her nerve endings from the intoxicating swirl of mint and cloves, a customized cologne she'd always adored. The lash of his body heat tempted her to look up, but she didn't move. His black loafers squeaked slightly as he walked around her. The anticipation built, fueling her adrenalin, and Cara fought the instinct to participate in the ritual. Years ago, she would've lifted her head to peek, or arch toward him for his touch. Not now. She'd learned the slow building tension only made the explosion more satisfying. She wanted desperately to show him how she'd changed.

His hand stroked her hair, lifting the strands and combing his fingers through it. A moan hovered on her lips. His touch was pure heaven, and she ached for more. "You cut your hair. Straightened it, too."

"Yes, Sir."

"I like it. The style suits you."

"Thank you, Sir."

He continued his inspection, his hands caressing her shoulders, exploring her firm flesh as he traced the line of her spine and drew goose bumps. He cupped her ass cheeks, pinching slightly, and then dipped one finger between her legs.

"You're wet."

Embarrassment hit, but she was already too turned on to care. Her pussy was swollen and tight. She loved being on display for him, ready to do what he commanded. The sheer freedom of giving herself over to this man who'd once held her heart in an iron grip coursed through her like a delicious drug.

"Do you like what I'm doing to you?"

His voice lashed like a whip, but his fingers were gentle as he swirled and rubbed her labia, gathering the moisture and coating her clit. Cara remained still, eyes half closed against the pleasure, fighting her body's reaction to ask for more. "Yes, Sir," she choked out.

"You used to fight me in this position. Said you didn't like being on your knees in front of me. Has this changed?"

"No, Sir."

"When I ask you a question, you will answer me honestly. Has this changed?"

Goosebumps broke out on her skin. "No, Sir. I liked it before. I was too afraid to admit it."

His grip tightened on her ass. Cara waited in the silence for his next move. She swore no matter how hard his questions were, she owed him her honesty. Tonight was not just about being physically naked, but emotionally. It was the driving force of what had been lacking in her life since she left Rem, and the craving for a Dom to challenge her on all levels haunted her continuously. Finally, tonight, she'd get what she wanted, but only if she was brave enough to give it.

"Forehead to the floor. Use your fingers to spread your ass cheeks wide. I want to see what belongs to me tonight."

He removed his fingers. A shudder shook her, but Cara dropped her forehead down to the carpet, and reached back to hold herself open to him. Arousal dripped down her inner thighs as she felt his blistering gaze study her pussy. She'd never felt more helpless. By him forcing her to present her body, he chained her tighter to his control and ratcheted her excitement.

"Your orgasms belong to me. Every single one of them. If you come without permission, you will be punished. If you do not obey my orders, you will be punished. Do you understand?"

"Yes."

"Yes, what?"

"Yes, Sir."

"I love you in this position. Offering your pretty pink pussy up to me to do whatever I want. I can touch you like this." His fingers swept over her weeping, swollen lips, stroking with merciless demand until she squeezed her eyes shut and locked her muscles to remain still. "Or use my tongue. Do you taste the same I wonder? Like soft, ripened peaches? Let's see."

Cara moaned with pleasure as his hot, wet tongue swiped her slit, gathering up her taste. He licked her with quick, teasing motions that hardened her clit and caused her hips to push back slightly for more. The sharp sting of his hand against her ass made her jerk. "Stay still." She panted for breath as he went back to licking her, until finally, mercilessly, he stood again and the squeak of his loafers hit her ears.

"Yes, still the same. Delicious."

Cara shook with the need for more. The need to come. She bit back her cries, knowing tonight was on his terms, and he'd just begun. Still, how long had it been since a man caused her to be this wet and achy after only a few moments? She craved an orgasm, dreamed of letting her body shatter until there was nothing left in her world but pleasure.

"I can see your clit begging for more. Do you want to come, Cara?"

"Yes, Sir," she gasped, her fingers curling into tiny fists.

"Tonight, you are my fuck toy. My gorgeous little slut. You will not come until I'm ready. Let's get back to the dirty little things I can do with your pussy. Ah, yes, I can spank it."

Oh, God.

Cara had always been a bit squeamish about certain BDSM play, but her body lit up like a firecracker at his casual statement. Would he spank her there? No, she was too vulnerable. No, she couldn't take it. She licked her lips. Say yellow? Or...

"Have you ever had your sweet pussy spanked, Cara?"

"No, Sir."

"Sometimes it throws a woman into orgasm. The shock of pain turns into hot pleasure. You will not come though, will you?"

Her thighs trembled and her fingers shook as she held herself open. "No, Sir." She held her breath, waiting for the sting, waiting for pain, but his fingers rubbed her labia in tiny circles, his thumb penetrating her in short, sharp strokes that ripped away her breath. So good. Her clit throbbed for pressure, and her cunt squeezed his finger, begging for more. "What a good little slut you are, wanting more. Like this, sweetheart?" He added another finger, giving just enough pressure. The world tilted as she hung on desperately for control, panicking at thought of her body breaking away from her.

"Yes, Sir," she gasped.

"And this?" Once again, his tongue worked her, flicking her clit, around and around, refusing to give her the flat of his tongue or the pressure needed to go over the edge. Frustrated tears stung her eyes. Cara didn't know such torture existed. Every ounce of need and want centered around her clit and the Holy Grail of orgasm. Her skin pricked with sweat, her nipples stabbed the carpet, her arms shook, and she swayed back and forth under the delicious licks of his tongue. "I asked you a question, Cara. Do you like my mouth on your pussy?"

"Yes, Sir, God, yes."

"You will not come."

The sharp sting of his open palm against her hard clit sent her over the edge. Pain jolted, then morphed into ecstasy. With a scream, her body jerked and she came hard, excruciating pleasure wracking her body in wave after wave. She shook under the violent spasms, and suddenly his arms were around her naked back. He soothed her with gentle caresses, down her spine, over her ass, her thighs, while he spoke in a dark, deep tone that touched a quiet place deep inside. Cara held her position with a ruthless determination, until he finally tugged her arms free, pulling her up from the floor and into his arms.

His scent surrounded her, and her cheek lay against the soft cotton of his t-shirt. Cara leaned in, accepting his warm strength. Flashbacks hit like stinging pebbles thrown at her.

The gentleness and love in his eyes when he held her after an orgasm. The way he'd tuck her tight into his body, wrapping his arms around her so she always felt safe and protected. Cherished. He was a man who could bring her to a ruthless orgasm, yet care for her with such shattering tenderness, her heart had never been able to escape the memory and belong to another.

The knowledge she still belonged to Remington Steele sliced through her with merciless precision. My God, no wonder her past relationships never amounted to more than a few dates or encounters. In a way, she'd always known she belonged to him. But being back in his arms confirmed the truth.

She was still in love with him.

"You disobeyed me, Cara," he whispered in her ear. The sweet caress of his hands over her body contradicted the hard promise in his voice.

"You've always had trouble controlling your orgasms. You still haven't met the Dom to correct this behavior?"

"No, Sir. It's just..." she trailed off, swallowing back the words.

"Finish your sentence."

"It's just with you."

He leaned back and tipped her chin up. Studied her face with hard eyes. "Do you think you can gain favor with me by pretty lies? I don't care how many men fucked you or how many times you came with them. But I won't tolerate lies."

She flushed but gave him back a stubborn glare. "I'm not lying. I have trouble orgasming with men. It's easier to do it myself."

Shock flared in those blue eyes. "You've obviously been trained in BDSM. You're trying to tell me your past Doms never brought you to orgasm? It's been five years since you ran from me. How am I supposed to believe this?"

"I've only been with a few other men. "

"Tell me about them."

"One man I was involved with for six months. He didn't really know the lifestyle. I got— frustrated. When I couldn't orgasm from regular intercourse without kink, he became upset and eventually ended it. The second said he liked BDSM and we built a friendship, but he wasn't a true Dominant. He enjoyed playing a bit, spanking, ordering me around. But again, I had trouble reaching orgasm and we ended it as friends. The third man is a practicing Dom who took me to his club, Chains. I decided I needed to go back into the lifestyle to find what I was looking for. I took an introductory course to learn the formal practices. You already taught me so much, but I needed more, on my own terms. Under his protection, I experimented and learned what I liked and what I didn't. He was only able to give me an orgasm with a vibrator. Not by his own hand."

"He never fucked you?"

"No, Sir. I haven't been able to come with another man since I left you."

Silence shattered the room. Cara knew he probed her gaze for truth, but there was nowhere to hide tonight. She'd hold nothing back with him. All of these years running from him had brought her right back into his arms.

"Then why are you here tonight?"

"To be free," she whispered. "I want to be pushed to my limits and beyond. I want to have orgasms and see if I can reach subspace with the right man. Tonight was the first time I intended to experience a full scene."

He stepped back, seemingly trying to sift through her words. It must sound farfetched, but the two other men who'd touched her had been pale imitations of the only one who owned her body and heart. She enjoyed the way her Dom teacher, Paul, brought her deep into BDSM, but she hadn't wanted him to fuck her. For her, it was learning what her body needed, and how far she wanted to push. Paul had respected her wishes.

No man had been able to set her off with a simple touch, like Rem.

Suddenly, he turned and towered over her. Blue eyes blazed with a mingle of emotions she'd never seen before, but his face was tight and his voice cold. "I think it's time we both share some hard truths, don't you? But first, I owe you a punishment. What do you think it should be, Cara?"

She swallowed but already knew the response. "Whatever you wish, Sir."

He nodded. "Very nice. And it shall be. Since you seem to like your orgasms and have little control, I think I'll indulge you." Nerves tingled and her heart stopped when his lower lip kicked up in a half smile. Danger shimmered from his presence. "I'll give you as many orgasms as you can handle."

Oh, no.

She stood frozen in place. Her belly fluttered with sweet anticipation and a hint of dread. She'd heard of this type of punishment before, but of course, Rem had never been too hard on her when they'd been together. No, he'd tried to show her the rules and be strict, but always indulged her when she protested too much.

But the Rem she knew was no longer here. The man before her had a different goal, to push her to the extreme limits of her endurance in order to find the deepest of pleasures and the surrender. Somehow, the threat added an intensity to the play that made her wet and aching. Cara longed to drop to her knees and service him; have him use her until he achieved his own satisfaction. The new Rem wasn't going to go easy on her. He wanted a strong woman who could hold her own.

It was time to show him how she'd grown and changed.

"Lie down on the bed spread eagled and wait for me."

His gaze challenged her to protest.

Cara dragged in a breath and went to the bed.

Chapter Five

REMINGTON FOCUSED ON UNZIPPING his black duffel bag, but his fingers shook around the tab. Fuck. He'd never been this thrown off in a scene before and he had to get his shit together. She'd always had a witchlike tendency to get him hard and fog his brain, and now he discovered nothing had changed. Watching her orgasm under the sting of his palm sent shock loads of satisfaction and possessiveness through his body.

She'd been magnificent. Giving herself up and over to anything he wanted, and letting her body take the orgasm it demanded. Cara never would've had the strength to deal with being so vulnerable. Their play had been tame when they were together, and he'd guided with a gentle hand, not wanting to scare her from the intense demands burning in his gut. Not wanting her to know about his true, dark cravings for domination and complete surrender.

For the first time, he didn't have to hold back. He could sink into his fantasy and give in to the raw hunger.

If only his emotions weren't ricocheting all over the damn place.

Five years. It was hard to believe her, but the truth reflected in her face in a way she couldn't hide. Cara hadn't come with another man. Why? Was she playing some type of game with him? Or had his memory haunted her in the same way?

No, he couldn't allow her to affect him. With another sub, he would've never held her after disobeying his command. He enjoyed being strict, but Cara's trembling body called to his. Rem had to hold her, comfort, stroke her soft skin and press her against his body. Her scent wrapped around him like a beautiful memory, the tang of fresh peaches, ripe and juicy and ready for his bite. He waited for her to say yellow and slow things down when he mentioned his punishment.

Instead, she'd walked to the bed without hesitation.

His dick wept for relief. His balls drew up tightly, straining behind his jeans. Rem hadn't been this uncomfortable in years. But tonight, finally, he'd take his pleasure. Take Cara any way he wanted, until he wrung the last drop of her essence out of his system. By morning, he'd be able to walk away without her memory haunting him.

First, though, he needed answers.

Rem withdrew the smooth leather ties from his bag, and fur lined shackles. Set the clitoral vibrator on the dresser. Condoms. Then turned.

God, she was beautiful. Her hands grasped the spindles of the headboard, legs spread wide apart, feet flat on the quilt. Her bright red hair spilled over the stark white of the pillow. The full curves of her body lay before him like a feast. White, unblemished skin tempted him to mark her with his hand. His belt. His dick.

Pushing back his desire to climb on the bed and fuck her senseless, he concentrated on tying both hands to the bed, and shackling her feet to each bedpost. He checked the fit, making sure she had enough space to allow circulation, then studied her face for any sense of discomfort. Her eyes grew a bit glassy, and her nipples were hard little points stabbing up into the air. The position allowed her wetness to gleam on her inner thighs, and her clit had poked from its hood, ready to play again.

Good. She was as turned on as he was. Wary, but not fearful. Exactly how he liked his sub.

Exactly how he liked Cara.

"Look at you spread out before me," he murmured, walking around the bed. "I can do anything I want. And what I want is to see you orgasm again. You're so pretty when you come, Cara. All flushed and trembling, wet and hot. You like to come, don't you?"

Her voice wobbled. "Yes, Sir."

Rem loved being fully dressed while she lay naked before him, like his spoils he could enjoy at leisure. Her body shook a bit in its bindings, and she tugged her wrists as if to check the hold.

"Oh, you're not going anywhere, sweetheart. Now, I'm going to give you this one for free. Come whenever you want. Enjoy."

Her eyes widened, and Rem almost chuckled at the wariness on her face. Of course, she'd find out soon enough. Orgasm torture was one of his favorite punishments, allowing him to both push his lover and exploit all of her sexual preferences in one shot. Also a lot of damn fun. He didn't know how Cara would respond, so he decided to begin slow and easy, then ramp her up.

Getting more comfortable for the fun ahead, Rem toed off his shoes and peeled off his t-shirt, throwing it to the side. The appreciation and lust in her gaze gave him a surge of satisfaction. He intended to satisfy her and block any other thoughts of other men, until her body wept for only his touch. Kneeling on the bed before her spread thighs, he began to stroke her slightly damp skin with long, slow caresses. From her ankles and up her legs, behind her knee to the hip, he re-learned the texture and sweep of her sweet body. Tweaking a hard nipple, he enjoyed her long moan as he cupped her heavy breasts and massaged, keeping pressure on the tips until she arched helplessly against him for more. She sucked in her belly as he ran a finger across the crease of inner thighs, skating over her bare, plump mound that demanded more.

"Has your body changed, Cara? Do you still like when I do this?" His thumb pressed lightly against her clit, flicking the nub back and forth until she writhed and pulled at her bonds. "Ah, yes, I see you do. What if I do this?" Rem lowered his head and licked her, scraping the edge of his teeth so gently against her clit her pussy wept. Breathing in her musky scent, he judged her already close to her second orgasm. Enjoying her open response, Rem stepped it up and curling his fingers, plunged three deep into her tight channel, curving to the right where her G-spot used to be. One thrust. Two. His lips closed around the throbbing nub and sucked hard.

She came against his mouth, hips jerking furiously, and he drew it out by sucking her even harder, his fingers mercilessly pushing her toward another peak. Twisting half of her body in a mingle of pain and pleasure, he kept up the intensity and was rewarded by her third orgasm, her voice hoarse as she screamed his name in helpless abandon.

Panting, she collapsed on the mattress. Licking his lips to gather up her delicious essence, he grabbed the vibrator to the side and turned it on low. The sound echoed but she was too far gone to register what was about to happen next.

"Beautiful, Cara. If you were mine, I'd lock you up and force you to come every hour. Your body was made for fucking. Even now, your juicy cunt wants more, doesn't it?"

"No! No more, Sir, please."

"Yes. Much more. Let's begin again."

Her moan stiffened his dick to the point of pain. He placed the humming vibrator against her sensitive clit, and her eyes flew open, shock carving out her face. "Oh, God, no."

"My name is Sir. If you want to beg for mercy, you do it to me."

He bent his head and sucked on a tight nipple, biting, licking, while he kept the vibrator against her nub, moving it around in slow circles so her entire clit got the full massage. Gasps escaped her swollen lips, and she flung her head back and forth in denial. She jerked and tried to avoid the vibrator, but Rem kept up the steady pace, moving to the other breast, pinching and licking until she was so sensitive, he bet she'd come from nipple play alone.

"Rem! Sir! I'm going to come again!"

"Good girl. Come for me."

He bit down on her nipple hard and ramped up the vibrator to its highest setting.

Cara came, bucking under his hold, and he laughed low, drinking in her beautiful face caught in up in ecstasy. In this moment, she was strong and open and real, more real than she'd ever been before when he'd promised her his heart, a ring, and his future.

She shook underneath him, and he dropped gentle kisses along her jaw, her temple, smoothing back her tangled hair. "Magnificent. But you're not done yet, are you sweetheart? There's more for me to take. More for you to give."

Pupils dilated, she slurred her words like a drunk. "Can't, Sir. Please, no more. Hurts."

He hardened his heart, telling himself she needed to be pushed to the edge. This was what they both needed, and he wouldn't be granting her fantasy if he didn't take her to the limit of her control. Rem soothed her with tender kisses, finally settling on that gorgeous mouth. Her lips were raw from being bitten, and he sipped from them gently, his tongue tracing the seam, dipping in for just a taste.

Her mouth opened.

He dove deep.

Rem groaned in sheer heaven as her familiar taste swamped his senses. Plunging his tongue in the dark, wet cave, he took with demand, fucking her mouth mercilessly until she gave him what she wanted and let him take her fully. The years melted away and his heart burst from his chest with the need to conquer; protect; own.

Until he reminded himself she was only his for the night.

He ripped his mouth from hers and stared into her face. "Beg me to come again, Cara."

"Noooo," she moaned, trying to fight him, a sob caught in her throat. "I can't."

"Try again. Unless you want to do this all night."

Rem watched. Waited. He prepared himself for the word yellow or red to burst from her lips. He couldn't blame her. Cara wasn't used to being pushed like other subs. She always hid behind excuses or fear of being completely naked with him, physically and emotionally. He hadn't cared when she belonged to him. He'd loved her with a raw passion worth everything. He'd been committed to teaching her to open up to her fantasies and allow him to protect her.

Rem locked up the messy emotions twisting through his body, his fingers poised to rip away the vibrator and call an end to the evening.

Irish green eyes met and held his, foggy with too much pleasure and the threat of more to come. The words came out ragged, in a whisper.

"Please, Sir. I'm begging for another orgasm."

Stunned, he locked his gaze on hers, making sure she wasn't too far gone to know what she was doing. The glint of determination and strength mirrored back excited him. Wrecked him. Humbled him.

Damn her. Damn her for making him want her this badly again.

"Very nice." This time he placed the vibrator deep inside of her, just brushing her clit with soft, slow strokes, bringing her back up the slippery slope back into full arousal. Rem took his time, tasting every inch of her skin as he pushed the instrument of torture in and out of her pussy. Her skin flushed, and her nipples pebbled. This time, instead of writhing and tearing at the bonds, she seemed to let go, accepting the tinge of pain from her swollen tissues, allowing herself to surrender back to the pleasure.

Rem slid back down her body, needing to get his mouth on her again. He played, using his tongue to lick and stroke her labia, her pussy, all the while fucking her deep with the vibrator. He gathered the wetness leaking from her thighs, humming under his breath dirty words that ramped up her arousal, watching her pretty pussy tighten and get ready again for another orgasm. Finally, she hovered on the edge, trying to fight it off but not able to control her body. Feeling like a fucking God, he lifted his head and watched her face, plunging the vibrator in and out, deeper and deeper, sliding just the right pressure against her sensitive clit and—

"Come for me, Cara."

She convulsed sobbing his name as she came again under his command. He reveled in the breaking apart of her body under his, smashing through the barriers, until there was nothing between them but honest need.

Tears leaked from her eyes but he wasn't done. Not yet.

"Please, Sir. Please don't make me do it again. I'm sorry. I'm sorry—"

"Once more. I need to be inside of you. I need to feel you clench around my dick. I need your last orgasm."

She shuddered. Rem put the vibrator on the edge of the bed and unbuckled his pants. Ripping the zipper down, he shrugged his jeans over his hips and quickly donned the condom. Even half wrecked, and over-sated, she watched him hungrily, gaze feasting on his dick like she wanted a taste.

He'd get to that later.

For now, he rose, his dick paused at her swollen, wet entrance. Now was the time. She was halfway gone into subspace, not able to tell pleasure from pain, and when all barriers were down truth became King.

"Why did you really leave me, Cara?" he growled. He pushed an inch into her pussy, avoiding her aching clit, not wanting to cause anymore pain until he got her back to the edge. "I want to know the real reason you left me some goddamn note on the bureau after years of belonging to me. Why you didn't talk to me? Tell me what was really going on? Why did you play me for a fool?"

She cried out, trying to reach out for him, trying to push him away. Her body took over and her hips arched for more. He pushed in another precious inch, giving her just a taste. "Oh, please. I loved you, Rem. I always loved you."

"Yet you left." Another inch. His fingers gripped her hips so hard he knew she'd wear his bruises in the morning. "You left and you're damn well going to tell me why."

Cara panted, eyes wild. "I was scared."

"Bullshit. I never would've hurt you. You were my whole fucking life. "

This time, he used his fingers to stimulate her clit. She screamed, trying to twist away but he was merciless, delving further into her delicious pussy, his eyes rolling back in his head with the brutal pressure of her channel squeezing his dick.

"It wasn't you, Rem! I didn't know if I could be the woman you needed me to be." He immediately pulled back, pausing to absorb her words. She struggled for breath. "You were always so sure of yourself. You knew what you wanted all the time and I was scared. I never had the time to figure out if I even wanted to be a sub because I loved you so much!"

He wrestled his iron-willed control and thrust inside her.

Her head flung back onto the pillow. Dear God, she was so tight and hot, he was gonna come in a flash. He grit his teeth and held on, feeling her body welcome him like he was finally home.

Her words hit his ears and his heart at the same time, drawing blood. No, it wasn't right. He'd never tried to make her anything she wasn't. He'd known how young they both were, and Cara never protested their play—never said she had any doubts during the endless conversations they'd had. He prided himself on open communication, lording it over the Doms he taught as key. How could he have failed at the one element that made him who he was?

"Why didn't you tell me?"

"Please, I can't, I can't come again."

"You will. Why didn't you talk to me?"

Cara sucked in a breath, shaking under the waves of sexual need gripping them both in a vise. The words that broke from her throat made him still above her, his cock buried deep.

"You didn't listen!" she cried brokenly "I tried to tell you I wasn't sure. But you were sure enough for both of us, so I ran. I ran because I was a coward, and I have to live with that for the rest of my life." She gulped, shaking violently underneath him. "Please, no more, no more."

"Come for me, Cara."

Without hesitation, Rem surged in and out, fucking her so completely, there was nowhere left to hide. His balls tightened up, and he pinched her clit, jerking up toward the right to hit her sweet spot, and then she was coming hard for him, and he let himself go.

Rem threw his head back and let the release wash over him in all its brutal force. Tremors grabbed him in a merciless grip, and he surrendered under the sheer force of ecstasy, spilling his seed, fucking the woman he'd once loved.

The woman he still loved.

Tears fell freely down her cheeks. Rem pressed his forehead to hers for a few precious moments, then left the bed. Unchaining her, he rubbed her ankles and wrists to get circulation back, then grabbed a bottle of water from the refrigerator. He sat on the edge of the bed and forced her to sit up halfway. "Drink this, sweetheart. That's it. You did well, I'm so proud of you." Between her tears, she gulped down the water, then lie quietly back on the pillows. Black mascara tracked down her cheeks. Her lips were red and bitten up. She was beautiful. Wrecked. Perfect.

His sub.

Rem went into the bathroom and dampened a washcloth. With gentle strokes, he cleaned the stickiness from her thighs, washed up, and returned to bed. She hadn't moved, just watched him with half dazed eyes that told him she was about to crash.

Rem shrugged off his jeans, and crawled underneath the crisp, white sheets. Gathering her in his arms, he tucked her head against his chest and held her close. Pressed his lips against her tangled hair. And waited.

The sobs shook her deep, coming from her soul, but he never broke his grip, and spoke to her gently, praising her, while he rained kisses over her wet cheeks until she finally settled.

Rem lay in the dark and remembered the day she had left.

He'd never forget the choking panic and fear when he'd come home and found all her stuff gone. His calls and texts went unanswered. Rem called the police like a crazy man, and his brothers had barely been able to calm him down until they found the brief note laid neatly on the nightstand he hadn't seen.

I'm sorry. I can't do this anymore. Forgive me.

Stupid. God, he'd felt so stupid when he realized she'd walked out on her own and he'd been the chump refusing to see the truth. How many days had he gone black, stumbling in a drunken fog of pain and loss? His brothers got him through it, but even now, Rem realized he'd never truly recovered from the way it ended. He never knew why. Endless nights caught up with torturous images of her with another man kept him from sleep. Finally, he forced himself to move on and forget her. Cara Winters was never coming back. Slowly, the pain was replaced by bitterness and anger, and when the memories hit, he learned how to bury them deep

As Cara fell into an exhausted slumber, he closed his eyes and wondered what he was going to do.

Chapter Six

*C*ARA WOKE UP WITH HIS arms wrapped tight around her.

She blinked, remembering the scene and the things she'd told him. Things she'd wanted to confess for a long, long time. Lying still, body sore from use, she wondered if Rem believed her. He was the type of Dom to always comfort a submissive. It was amazing how ruthless he could be within a scene; trained completely on her satisfaction no matter what he used to get her there. He'd changed. Before, if she protested, or sulked, or fought his demands, he gave in. Cara knew it was because he'd loved her and recognized they were finding their way.

But it had still been too much for her.

"You're awake."

She blinked and lifted her gaze. Stunning ocean blue eyes seethed with a variety of emotions, before shutting down behind the barrier. Cara knew the wall too well. She'd used it many times in her past, but not tonight. Tonight, was a gift, and she'd use the opportunity without holding back.

"Yes. I'm sorry about—that."

A frown marred his dark brows. "Never be sorry about emotion. It's the most honest thing we have. My intent was to push you to tears. Sometimes, we need the cleansing. How are you feeling?"

"Good. A bit sore."

"Good. I always liked you sore. Meant you were worshipped the way you should be."

Raw emotion clogged her throat. This man had never left her heart, even after all these years. The combination of ruthless command and aching gentleness undid her completely. She spoke in a husky voice. "Rem, I should've never ran away. I didn't want to hurt you, but I convinced myself it would be better for both of us if I just disappeared."

His jaw clenched. "Better for you, Cara. Not me. I have to hand it to you—I had no idea. I thought you were as happy as I was."

"You did make me happy. But I doubted myself, and each time I tried to share with you, you told me I was perfect." Misery crept through her. "It's crazy, I know, but I needed you to step back and let me find my way. It wasn't just about the sex, Rem. You were sure about your future as a dealer, and our future. Sure about your wants, and your needs. You knew where we were going to live, and that I'd work as a teacher, and that we'd have three children one day. There was never any room for doubt, and I felt like, I felt like—"

"Like what?"

She dragged in a breath and dove into truth. "I felt like I was disappearing. I didn't know who I was anymore, because you already knew. Does that make sense?"

Naked pain flickered over his face. Cara reached out and touched his cheek. He flinched. "Yes. I loved you too much."

Cara closed her eyes against the grief. "Yes. I wasn't ready for a man like you. I needed to crash and burn and make mistakes and find out who I was. Without you."

The distance and coolness shimmered around him. Cara felt as if she could actually touch the barrier separating them, from too many regrets and scars that never healed properly. It was her fault. He hadn't deserved to spend these past five years wondering what he'd done wrong. Somehow, some way, Cara needed to heal this man, and forge something new between them. They couldn't go back.

But they could move forward.

"Rem, I thought about contacting you, but I was afraid I'd beg your forgiveness and re-start the cycle. I had to grow up and find my own way first. I never stopped loving you."

His lips tightened. "Cara, you were never returning to me. And I couldn't take you back. The cliché is exactly right – there's too much water under this bridge to save. What you love is the memory of your first love. But it wasn't real."

Her eyes stung. "Yes, it was," she said. "It was so real it scared the living hell out of me. Don't you know why I signed up for FANTA-C, Rem? I wanted to experience everything I'd ever been afraid of. You were right. I'm a submissive, and I love that part of myself. I just wasn't ready to be your submissive. Now, I know I'm the woman I always knew I could be. Not a girl, but a woman to hold her own and not be afraid when things get hard. A woman strong enough to be yours."

Rem shook his head. "What we had is long gone. You've haunted me over the years. I think we were meant to see each other one last time to clear up the past. Maybe we can finally let each other go now."

Cara jerked back. Of course. He looked at this night as a cleansing to wring her from his system. She didn't blame him. All she could do is give him everything he asked for and more. Surrender her body and her heart and soul. If she lost, at least she had no regrets.

"Rem, you're not alone. I've woken up every morning with the memory of your face behind my closed lids. I've gone to sleep every night with your name on my lips."

In seconds, he roared up and flipped her over, pinning her arms back and pressing her deep into the mattress. She gasped at the leashed savagery of his hold, the thick strain of his cock pressing against her buttocks. Primal desire pumped through her veins and made her wet.

"I'm not here to talk about the past," he growled in her ear. "I'm here to test your limits. I'm here to fuck you over and over until dawn. Understood?"

She shivered and kept her secret close to her heart. Everything made sense now. These last five years had been necessary to make her way back to him, and gain his forgiveness. She'd win him back. She had no choice, but right now, he was her Dom and demanded her submission. "Yes, Sir."

"Good. Get up from the bed and wait for my instructions."

He climbed off her. Cara stood beside the bed, naked. She made sure to keep her shoulders back and spread her legs. His nod of approval made her confidence surge.   Cara watched him rustle a spreader bar from his duffel bag, along with two long chains. Her eyes widened in surprise when he walked to the center of the room and attached the chains to the hooks in the ceiling.

His lip kicked up in that famous half smile. "FANTA-C has these hotels for a reason. I told them exactly what I needed for tonight, and they provided." He tested the hold and made some adjustments. "Come here, Cara."

She obeyed. He shackled each of her wrists. Her hands were pulled above her head, but not too high where she'd cramp up. "Feet wide apart, please." Cara spread her legs wide, and he slipped the spreader bar between her ankles. Once again, he adjusted the width until she was open to him but her thighs weren't straining with discomfort. The position put her completely at his mercy, her body on display for whatever he wanted to do.

The slow, smug grin curved his lips. How badly she wanted that delicious mouth on her everywhere. The memory of those powerful orgasms tightened her nipples into hard points, and immediately, her pussy throbbed in demand. Remington Steele was addictive. Her body had never forgotten him, and was well trained in responding to the slightest touch or look.

"Very nice. Does anything hurt?"

"No, Sir."

"We'll fix that soon." Her heart pounded frantically as he removed a flogger. Smacking it against his palm, the thud of the leather hit her ears and flooded her with arousal. "Ah, I see someone has learned to enjoy the flogger. Who was the Dom that trained you?"

"Paul, Sir."

Determination flickered in his eyes. "I know Paul well. Let's see how well he served you, shall we? I'll begin with a warm-up. Don't forget your safe word."

"Yes, Sir."

Cara began the deep breathing she was taught, and softened her body against the dull slap of the flogger. He kept a light, experienced hand, covering every inch of skin until she was warm and tingly. She pulled at the chains, enjoying her bondage and the sound of the clinking metal, reminding her all choices were out of her hand. Rem circled her body, moving from the back of her legs, up to her ass, and covering her back. Suddenly, his hard hands were on her ass, rubbing and squeezing her flesh, dipping one finger into her pussy to test her wetness. A moan spilled from her lips.

"You're so wet, sweetheart. My little slut likes to get beaten by my hand. I like my subs vocal. So I won't be satisfied until you scream, Cara. Until you beg me to let you come. Do you understand?"

She gasped as his finger coated her clit with her own wetness. A tingle of alarm cut through her. She disliked yelling during a flogging, preferring to bury the pain deep inside. To her, it was a test of her will. A matter of dignity. But he wanted her agreement, so she easily gave it to him. "Yes, Sir."

"Let's begin."

Cara jerked at the first real slap against her ass. The sting was more than she anticipated, and her body tensed up. God, it hurt. Paul had moved slowly, taking her to higher levels with a careful precision that allowed her to trust. If Paul gave her a hard slap, his next would be medium, then low, then back up. It became almost hypnotic and soothing. She'd heard many subs found a deep release via the use of pain, and though she enjoyed it, Cara figured she wasn't built that way.

Rem continued without lessening the strength of his hits. She liked the flogger. But not like this. Not with such...intensity. She waited for a breather, but Rem fell into a steady rhythm, alternating right to left, increasing the blows until she was shaking with the effort not to wriggle away. Swallowing hard, she tried to wrap her mind around the pain and sift through it. Biting her lip hard, she struggled to remain quiet.

The next blow on her inner thigh forced a low cry from her throat. A strange, unsettled emptiness rose up from her belly, flickering across her sensitive nerve endings. Her ass burned like fire.

Suddenly, he stopped. "I'm not hearing you, Cara. Where are we? Do you need your safe word?"

She panted and squeezed her eyes shut. "No, Sir."

"Open your eyes."

His gaze trapped hers, pinning her harder than his body had on the bed. Something shook loose inside, but she was desperate to shove it back.

"You will not suffer in silence, sweetheart. You will give me your voice. Your pain. Your screams. I'll keep you safe, but you have to let go first." His face gentled, but his eyes gleamed with implacable demand. "Don't suffer the pain, or fight it. Breathe with it, embrace it, and you'll be carried to the other place. Do you understand?"

Cara heard the words but struggled to believe him. "Yes, Sir."

His lips tightened, catching her in the lie. "We'll begin again."

Oh, God.

The blows came faster and harder. Cara fought the intense sensations and the warring emotions growing inside of her. His lashes never wavered, striking perfectly over each ass cheek, the back of her thighs, the sensitive crease near her pussy. Hot tears burned her lids, and she tasted blood on her bitten lip. An odd throbbing sensation beat from between her thighs, demanding release, until arousal and pain mingled to a razor sharp edge where she couldn't' recognize one from the other. She would not cry for mercy. She would not cry. She would not—

She jerked in her bonds as the last lash caught her across the center of her ass. Color burst behind her closed lids, and her mouth opened and she was yelling, letting her voice finally escape.

"Please, oh, God, Rem, please!"

"Good girl. Let it go, sweetheart." His fingers delved into her soaked pussy, thrusting in and out, scraping against her clit, and Cara went wild underneath him, not able to keep her reserve or hold back. Sobbing his name over and over, she begged him to let her come, her hips helplessly jerking back and forth, trying to ride his fingers. "Fuck, you're dripping, your body loves it. I need more."

"No, please let me come, please!" she cried.

"I can take you further. I *will* take you further."

Hanging on the edge of a shattering orgasm, he began flogging her again, but this time she didn't fight the blows. With tears streaming down her cheeks, she yelled for him, screamed his name, begged him for mercy, all the while her body tightened and shook with raw need to shatter under his hands. Caught in the violent grip of agonizing pleasure, she hung there, waiting on his command. Each blow pushed her toward freedom, her mind and body locked on one thing only—to come. For him.

A distant part of her mind registered Rem had dropped the flogger. He dropped to his knees before her, head thrown back, fierce satisfaction glowing in his eyes. As she hung before him, open and vulnerable, she felt as powerful and adored as a sexual goddess, and a throaty roar escaped her lips, echoing in the room like an animal ready to mate.

"Fucking magnificent. Fucking perfect. Now, I want you to come for me, Cara. Come hard."

His mouth buried into her pussy the same time his hands grabbed her ass and squeezed.

Pain and pleasure collided and thrust her into orgasm.

Cara screamed and surrendered to the agonizing convulsions of ecstasy. His mouth took it all, devoured her whole, and every inch of her body clenched and let go in one dizzying flow of release. Caught up in the violent waves, she heard his dim shout, and then he was fucking her, deep and hard, gripping her bruised hips and marking her as his, only his, forever his.

Time stopped. Time passed.

She slumped in her chains, boneless. Gentle hands freed her from the bonds, and she was carried over to the chair. A warm blanket wrapped around her. Cara snuggled into the delicious warmth, the intoxicating scent of mint and cloves drifting to her nostrils. He rocked her, pressing kisses against her temple, hugging her tight. Cara fell into a cocoon of safety, and for the first time, connected with a part of her she hadn't known existed. The part buried way deep inside, that still hung on to her negative thoughts, and fears. That hung onto the voices telling her she wasn't good enough. And finally, Cara realized all was quiet inside her, like a temple of peace within her own body.

"I still love you," she slurred, leaning her cheek against his shoulder. "I will always love you."

Then she slept.

Chapter Seven

*R*EM STARED AT THE CLOCK.

Six am.

The night was officially over.

As if she sensed his thoughts, Cara shifted in his arms, muttering something under her breath. A smile touched his lips. God, she was beautiful. Always had been, but over the years, she'd ripened into a woman with strength and fortitude. She knew who she was, and it was the sexiest thing in the world. The way she submit to him last night would haunt him forever, and Rem wondered if he'd ever be able to accept any less. He'd be comparing all future women to Cara. The night that was supposed to banish her ghost had done the exact opposite.

Rem didn't think he'd ever get over her.

She frowned in sleep and he bent his head to press a kiss in the deep furrow of her brow. She settled, and he studied the fall of her Titian hair, the gentle curve of her cheek, the swollen fullness of her strawberry lips. Finally, he knew what it meant for a woman to give him everything. She'd be wearing his marks today, and his dick immediately hardened at the thought. Last night, he'd rubbed cream into her skin, soothing away the sting, then fucked her again. Slow. Quiet. He commanded her not to make a sound, and it only made it more exciting. Watching her shatter around him with a soundless cry on her lips pushed him to the limit. The intimacy between them was more than he'd ever had with another woman after only a few precious hours. Rem craved to roll her over, spread her thighs, and thrust in deep. One last time to savor her orgasm; the bite of her nails; the throaty scream of his name breaking from her lips.

Instead, he had to say good-bye.

His chest tightened. Her raw honesty had carved a wound in his heart, but Rem understood so much more now. In his mind, he'd been doing his job. Taking care of his lover, his sub, giving her everything she needed. He assumed confidence and security and encouragement would help her blossom. But she'd been too young. How could he possibly blame her for trying to find her own way? Make her own mistakes? If they'd only met a few years later, Rem knew they'd probably would've been married and lived happily ever after.

Maybe it just hadn't been fated.

He still hated her methods of leaving him, with only a note to torture himself with for years. But in the buried truth in his soul, Rem understood now. In her mind, there was no other way. If Cara had run back to him and tried to explain, Rem wondered if he would've done exactly what she was afraid of. Take her back, chain her with sex, and promise to make her happy.

He hadn't seen what she really needed.

Grief beat through him. He'd failed her. And all these years hating her; loving her; twisted raw emotions that made no logical sense and pushed him to try and forget her, Rem realized he'd come full circle.

FANTA-C had brought them back together for a second chance.

But Rem couldn't do it.

God, he wished they had a shot to start over. But the past was too big for him to get past. One night wasn't enough to cleanse his soul and allow him to begin again. There was still too much disappointment for his inability to make her truly happy years ago. And who knows if he could ever make the new Cara happy? He didn't know what she wanted or needed anymore. It was a blueprint for disaster.

"Rem?"

Her husky voice raked across his ears. He stared down, stroking her tangled hair back from her face, and smiled. "Hey, sweetheart. How do you feel?"

"Good. Tired. Happy." She smiled back. "Sated."

"Then I did my job. I'll run you a bath to soak your sore muscles."

"Will you stay?"

He jerked back. His new Cara was ruthlessly, honest and direct. Pride filled him, along with a deep sadness that rivaled Eyore. He'd wanted to spoil her for a bit before walking away. But maybe this was better. Cleaner. How could he fight his instinct to make her his one more time? It would be too dangerous.

He may decide never to leave.

"No," he said. "I'm not staying, Cara."

She raised her chin. Those meadow green eyes glinted with resolve. "Why not? I'm asking you to please think about giving us a try. I want to know who you are today. I know we can never be what we were, Rem. I ruined that for both of us. But maybe we can be something even better."

He couldn't take the searing hope in her eyes, so he got out of bed and pulled on his jeans. "I can't. Last night was special to me. Being with you again was amazing. But I failed you before, and damned if I'm going to do that again."

Rem jerked back as a pillow hit his back. WTF?

She stood beside the bed, naked, shaking with anger.

"Don't you dare give me that shit, Remington Steele!" she shot back. "You didn't fail anyone. I was the one who ran away and chose not to talk to you. I can't erase the past, but I'll be damned if

I allow you to blame yourself. You loved me well. I just wasn't ready."

His gaze narrowed. His dick hardened and throbbed. Holy shit, she was magnificent. Naked, trembling, eyes lit with fire, her white skin held an array of pinkish marks he'd put on her. "Don't throw another pillow at me, woman. It was my responsibility to figure out if something bothered you. I should've known you were pulling away and unhappy. I have to live with that. I don't want to hurt you, but this needs to end with last night."

"No."

He shook his head. "What did you just say to me?"

In pure shock, he dodged the next pillow launched at his head. Cara was mischievous but never would've dared to throw something at him. "This doesn't have to end unless you're too much of a coward to try," she said. "Don't do what I did, Rem. Don't run from this."

Anger shook through him. How dare she question his motives and challenge his decision? With one yank, his jeans came back down. "Beg me for forgiveness, right now, Cara. Or you'll regret it." His Dom voice usually left her apologetic and a bit humbled.

This time, the third pillow hit his shoulder.

"Fuck you!"

"Oh, I will, little girl. You asked for it." She bit her lip, looking for an escape route. Adrenalin flooded his body and his cock was so damn hard it could cut stone. "Run, and it'll be worse."

She ran.

Good. He was looking forward to this.

He launched himself across the bed and snagged her around the waist. Holding on to her wriggling, naked body, she screeched in protest as he threw her down and pinned her to the mattress. He held her wrists in one hand while he quickly donned the condom. Not wasting any time, he pushed her legs open with his thigh, and took her with one strong thrust.

"Oh, God!"

"Fuck, you're so wet," he grit out. "This one's for me, little brat."

Rem fucked her hard and long, holding her arms above her head. This time, it was a simple claiming, a reminder of who was in charge and who she belonged to. In seconds, she was writhing beneath him, looking for more, her hard nipples stabbing against his bare chest in demand. Her pussy clenched around his dick and with one last plunge, he came hard, jerking his hips to spill the last of his seed, roaring her name in satisfaction.

Fully sated, he pulled out and slipped off the condom. Her body was flushed, and her arousal lay sticky on her thighs. Her clit peeked out, dying for attention.

"Very nice."

He climbed off the bed and she sat up, eyes wide with astonishment. "What? You can't leave me like this!"

He frowned. "I'd advise you to remember you got in this position for mouthing off. And throwing pillows."

"Please, Rem. I need you."

Her soft voice trembled with need, and her beautiful body was ripe for the plucking. Rem stood, feet braced apart, and motioned her.

"On your knees. Show me how much you need me."

Cara scrambled off the bed and dropped to her knees. Her gaze trained on him, she waited for permission. Satisfaction cut through him. She was so perfect. Finally, he nodded. "Suck my cock. Make me come again."

She cradled his dick with warm, gentle hands, stroking and teasing from root to tip, then lowered her mouth and took him deep.

Ah, shit.

It was heaven. It was hell. Her wet mouth sucked him tight, and her fingers caressed and squeezed his balls in perfect rhythm. He rocked his hips back and forth, and almost immediately, he grew back to full length. Bumping the back of her throat, she hummed around his cock, breathing through her nose and taking him all in, until he went crazy and grabbed her head, making her fuck him with short, hard thrusts.

He exploded in her mouth, coming down her throat, and she swallowed, licking him clean, before sitting back on her heels. Rem groaned and gripped her chin, looking down at her.

Her face reflected a pure joy from serving him. Pure need from wanting him. And pure grace for surrendering.

"Sir? I'm begging you..."

He struggled for breath. "For what? State your need."

"I'm begging you to fuck me, Sir. I need you inside me."

Rem broke.

With a groan, he pushed her down on the carpet, grabbed another condom, and slid home. This time, he made sure she came fast and hard. With expert strokes, he rubbed her clit continuously until she fell into another orgasm, breaking apart in the grip of his arms.

When they finally collapsed, she asked him again. "Stay with me, Sir. Give us one more chance."

His eyes half closed and he fought the war inside him that screamed for him to give in. To try. But he didn't trust himself not to blur the past with the present. What if he scared her off again and he found himself hurt? This time, he'd never recover. There'd be no hope of picking up the pieces.

No, he had to walk away with a perfect memory. At least, he finally knew the truth and could begin to heal from the past.

"I can't," he said softly. "I don't want either of us to be hurt again, Cara."

Her eyes filled with tears and a broken understanding that ripped him apart. "I learned another thing through the years, Rem. Life is messy. There's no guarantees. I'm okay with it now, because the trade-off is worth everything. But I can't do it alone. You have to want me as bad as I want you."

"Cara—"

"It's okay. I understand." She forced a smile. "May I ask you to please, leave? I need some time alone."

His emotions warred. His gut ached to give in and stay, but his mind locked down and forced his body to leave the bed and get dressed. He paused at the door, his fingers wrapped around the knob.

"Are you sure you're okay?"

"Yes. Good-bye, Rem. Thank you for last night. I'll never forget it."

"Neither will I." He dragged in a breath and opened the door. "Good-bye, Cara."

He left the room with an emptiness and searing pain, telling himself over and over it was all for the best.

Chapter Eight

"**W**AIT A MINUTE. YOU SAW CARA? Cara was your one night stand?" Rafe asked in disbelief.

Rem sipped his coffee and regarded his brothers. They always had brunch on Sundays, which was a good time to catch up, recover from any hangovers and pig out. Rome was ignoring his giant stack of banana pancakes, fork poised mid-flight. Rick stared, mouth half-open like a guppy.

"You guys didn't know anything about this, right?"

Rick shook his head. "Dude, we'd never do that to you. The reason we set up FANTA-C in the first place was to help you get over her. What the hell is she doing in Vegas?"

Rem rubbed his forehead. "I don't know," he admitted. "Not sure if I even asked her. The night was like a whirlwind. "

Rafe propped his elbows on the table. "Did you sleep with her?"

Rem nodded.

"Are you back together?" Rick asked.

"No. She asked me to give her another chance, but it's too much for me."

Rome tapped the table with his finger. "How do you feel about her? Do you want to try again? Did she tell you why she left?"

Rem gave him the brief run-down on Cara's explanation. "I blame myself. I should've known how unhappy she was. Fuck, she had to run away from me in order to be heard. What type of Dom am I? What type of lover am I?"

Rick turned hard eyes on him. "First off, you were in love and would've died for Cara. You're not a mind reader. None of us are. We can only help our women if they tell us the truth, and that's been the downfall of a ton of relationships. Does Cara blame you?"

"No, she blames herself."

"I still hate the way she did it," Rome said. "But I think you were both at fault. Being a martyr though, doesn't help the situation, bro. You can't change the past, but you can damn well make sure you have open communication in the future. Did you like being with her again?"

It had only been two nights since he left her, and already he felt like he was slowly going out of his mind. He caught her scent around each corner. He'd followed two strange women already because the swing of their hips and shot of red hair reminded him of Cara. He was a wreck, but he hoped with enough time, he'd settle.

Rem groaned. "Hell, yes, I loved being with her. But I'm not up for this shit again. She has this spell over me. I just look at her and I'm hard and all I want to do is fuck her and protect her and make her happy."

Rome winced. "Yep, I feel that way about Sloane. You're done, dude. You still love her."

Rafe nodded. "That's the exact feeling I get about Summer. I don't think it goes away. Believe me, I tried."

Rem looked at his last brother.

"Tara is my life," he said simply. "And if you feel half of what I do for Tara, I wouldn't let her go, bro."

Rem finished his coffee and shook his head. "I can't. It was an amazing night, but it's over. Too many ghosts are between us. If I screwed up once, I can do it again."

"Or maybe you've both learned enough to make it work."

Rem ignored Rome's Yoda comment. "It's better this way."

His brothers shared a meaningful look. "What if you run into her?" Rafe asked.

"Doubt it. Vegas is big, and we don't run in the same circles." Except the BDSM club she'd mentioned. That nugget of information had been bothering him like a grain of sand in his shoe, rubbing him slowly raw. "Hey, anyone know Paul at Chains?"

Rick and Rafe nodded. "Yeah, he's a Dom. Does teaching and introductory classes. You know him?"

Remington shifted in his seat. Fuck. The idea of going into Chains and finding Cara with another Dom filled him with frustration. And anger. He tried to swallow it back. "Seems Cara has been going to Chains to be trained. She said Paul is her teacher."

Rick waved his hand in the air. "Paul is very good at knowing what a sub needs to be comfortable. He usually doesn't have sex with his trainees unless they specifically request it. He's a good guy. Knows his stuff. Still, I'm surprised I haven't seen Cara before. She was probably receiving private lessons."

Rem relaxed. Cara had been telling the truth. She'd learned so much, he figured she had tons of Doms after him, but maybe it had always been just him. Damn, he'd loved being the man to give her multiple orgasms and push her limits. Making her come was addictive. "Thanks. Umm, if you happen to see her at Chains, just let me know."

Rick frowned. "So you can go apeshit on us? Rem, are you sure you're ready to give her up for the second time?"

Rem threw a few bills on the table. "I'm sure. I gotta go."

As he walked out of the restaurant, his brothers' stares called him a liar.

***

Cara stood on the edge of the casino and watched Rem work.

It had been two weeks since their night together. Two weeks of sheer misery and crying and regrets. She understood why he didn't want to try again. But last night, after talking to her girlfriend, the light bulb had switched on and blinded her with a startling revelation.

Years ago, she'd left him. She hadn't fought for their relationship, or tried to reach out to tell him the truth.

This time, she had to be the one to make a stand. For her. For him.

For them.

Deep inside, Cara knew she had the strength to fight. It was time for Rem to see she wasn't giving up. He was still under the illusion she was the type of girl to slink away after losing the battle.

But Cara was a full-grown woman now. And she was going to win the war.

She'd dressed carefully in a simple dark green dress in a stretchy knit that gave under her generous curves. A hint of cleavage was revealed with the V neckline, and a gold chain belt cinched her waist. Her heels were four inch black stilettos. Her hair was twisted up in a loose knot, allowing strands to frame her face and soften the severity.

His shift ended at midnight.

Cara would be waiting.

Right on cue, he switched out with the new dealer, shutting down his station and nodding to the players. His crisp black pants and white shirt hugged his lean figure, and as soon as he left the floor, his fingers were loosening the top buttons and rolling up his sleeves. His long strides ate up the casino floor, and Cara stumbled to catch up.

He had just turned around the flashing game of Sex in the City, when she picked up her speed and bashed right into a hard chest.

Uh, oh.

Her eyes widened as he stared down at her with chilly blue eyes. Damn, he was pissed. She probably should've yelled his name instead of trying to stalk him, and now he thought she was one of those crazy exes.

"What are you doing, Cara?" he demanded.

She swallowed, threw her head back, and went for it. "Coming to see you. Wanted to check if you'd like to grab dinner."

His eyebrow shot up. "It's midnight," he said mildly. "A little late for dinner, don't you think?"

"I know after work, no matter how late it was, you always craved a big meal."

"I don't think it's a good idea," he said.

Cara meant to give her rehearsed speech, but instead found herself babbling. "I don't want to make a pest out of myself, and I respect your decision not to continue our relationship. But I want to get to know you again. As friends."

"Friends?"

"Yes, friends." She stumbled over the word and heard her inner voice scream LIAR. She ignored it. "It's rare to have someone in your life who knew who you really were. God, Rem, I had dinners with your family, and hung with your brothers. I dragged you to art galleys and you forced me to sit through football games. But we were friends before we were lovers. Can't we just have a meal together and talk? No sex. No intensity. Just...talk?"

Her shoulders tensed as she waited. If this didn't work, she'd need to compose a plan B, but Cara hoped he'd be curious enough to give her this. She watched the mingle of emotions flicker over his face. Cara stood her ground. Kept her gaze on his. And waited.

"Okay?"

She jerked back. "Really?"

That half smile curved his lips and her heart did a slow flip-flop. "Really. But no trying to seduce me at the table."

She grinned back. "Deal. Pasta or steak?"

"Pizza. Lots of it."

"You still like ham and pineapple?"

"Damn straight."

She shuddered. "I still hate it."

They laughed and headed over to the fast food section, where a brick oven specialty shop served up personalized pies with a variety of toppings. Rem grabbed a Sam Adams Octoberfest, a Blue Moon for her, two Hawaiian slices, and one plain. They slid into a red vinyl booth with paper plates and drank beer from the bottle. Familiarity settled around them.

"Why'd you say yes?" she asked, taking a sip of the cold, citrusy brew.

He shook his head. "You're direct. I like that."

"You deserve that," she said softly.

Surprise flickered in his eyes. He nodded. "I said yes cause I'm hungry and you've been on my mind. I thought sharing a meal would be...nice."

"I'm happy you've been thinking of me. I've been replaying that night in my mind over and over these past weeks. But I haven't been feeling...nice."

His gaze narrowed. "You agreed no sex."

She bit her lip in guilt. "You're right. My bad. Tell me about your brothers. I've missed them. Are they all here in Vegas with you?"

Rem probed her face to make sure she really felt guilty, and then bit into his pizza. "Yeah, they came out here one by one until they finally recruited me a few months ago. It's nice working with them again, though. We're trying to get Mom and Dad out here for a long vacation."

"How are your parents?" she asked. She still remembered the warmth and chaos in the household brimming with boys. Rem's mom ruled with an iron hand, and a lot of food. Sunday dinners were a staple, with football on in the background, crowded at the dining room table, hosting meatball eating contests. Cara always felt like she was truly home in the Steele house.

"Good. Dad retired so they're having fun being on their own schedule. Traveling."

"Are any of your brothers married?"

He shook his head. "Not yet. But they're all in committed relationships right now and seem happy. It's nice. Rafe got out of the military so it's good to have him home safe."

Cara sighed. "You have such a tight knit family. I'm glad you're all back together."

"Your turn. How'd you settle on Vegas? Or are you?"

"I am. Bought a little house outside of town. After I left Atlantic City, I headed down south. I craved the sun and the feeling of everything being a bit lighter. I did some odd jobs for a while, waitressing, book store clerk, and then finally I realized I really wanted to go back to school."

"For history? Teaching?"

"Special education. I love it. I always felt something didn't fit with being a professor, or even teaching elementary. But once I began working with special needs children, something clicked. I finished my degree, and decided to head for California to settle. But there were some great opportunities in Vegas, so I tweaked my plan, came here, and fell into the world immediately."

"Vegas isn't too much for you?"

She laughed. "That's what I love about it. You can come to the Strip and have all your desires met. But I have a great job, and live in a really quiet neighborhood, so it's like the best of both worlds."

"You always did hate the winters," he murmured. "You'd wear those godawful socks in neon colors. They were so thick they rivaled my grandmother's."

"Cold feet, warm heart," she recited.

They smiled at each other, and the crackle of electricity zinged in a crazy loop, pulling them a bit closer. She studied the carved features of his face, heavy brows, square chin, the spill of coal hair over his forehead. God, he was so beautiful. God, she wanted him so much.

Instead, she veered back to friendly topics of conversation. She needed him to learn to trust her again. Not the Cara from years ago, but the woman she'd become. They'd already bonded physically, but now, she needed to see if Remington Steele could also like her.

"You still play the guitar?" she asked.

"Hell, yes. I jam by myself usually, but Rick hooked me up with three other guys who like to play. We meet once a week."

"I'm glad. There was something about you when you played guitar."

"I looked cool, right? You wanted me?"

Cara laughed. "I always wanted you, Rem. No, it was this sense of freedom. Pure joy in your face. I could watch you for hours."

He tilted his head and studied her. "The last few women I dated rolled their eyes and called me a Peter Pan. They didn't get it."

"They didn't get you."

The jolt of connection sizzled. He pulled his gaze away, and took a long pull of his beer. "Tell me about your teaching. Rafe's girlfriend teaches at Lakeside Elementary."

"Great school. I actually work for a private institution. Sommerset Park. The classes are small, and I have a lot of support. I feel like I can do my job well. Get to know the kids on a personal basis."

"Do you still volunteer at animal shelters? Take in strays?"

"I do. I spend Saturdays helping out, and fostering senior dogs when I can."

"Remember those feral cats you were determined to help? They scared the hell out of me. Yet, they came to you like you were their mother."

Her eyes glowed from the memory. "They were born under the front porch. The poor mother was so scared. It took me forever to get her to trust me."

"She used to hiss and snarl when I came to visit you."

Cara giggled. "Such a big, bad, Dom. You used to wait in the car and call me out because you were afraid to come in."

He glowered. "I've heard of mother cats killing men before to protect their young."

"At least I got them all homes eventually."

"You always did want to save the world," he murmured.

Cara gave a long sigh. "I learned I can't. But if I take it one by one, I can make a small difference."

"You made a difference to me."

She reached out and took his hand. His strong fingers closed around hers. "Sometimes, when we're like this, it feels like yesterday. Doesn't it?"

He nodded and squeezed her hand. "Yes. But it's not."

"That's better," she said. "I wouldn't want what we had before."

"Was it that bad?"

She flinched and glared. "Of course not! But we're not the same people, and we owe ourselves something bigger and better."

"Cara—"

"But I just want to be friends."

"So you said. How does this friendship thing work?"

She gave a cheeky grin, knowing she had a shot at this. Rem wanted an excuse to see her, so she'd give it to him. "No sex, of course. We hang out and do some fun stuff together. No pressure."

His brows snapped in a frown. Cara giggled as frustration simmered around him. Obviously, he hated not being in control of this relationship, but it was the only way to get his guard down and allow him to really see her. "I don't know."

"Will you give it a try?" she asked seriously. "Please?"

He considered. Cara knew Rem took his time with problems. His sharp intellect allowed him to look at the issue from different angles before making a decision. She figured she'd have to wait it out, but suddenly, he gave her the answer.

"Okay. I'll try."

She beamed at him. "Thanks."

His slow smile warmed her heart and gave her hope.

There was still a chance.

Chapter Nine

"*F*UCK! HE PEED ON MY LEG!"

"Oh, he didn't mean it. Harry just smelled the other dogs on you. He gets confused."

Rem stared at the mottled mutt staring adoringly up at Cara. And then he saw it. She scratched his ears, turned, and Harry shot him a disgusted, snotty look. The dog practically sneered before flicking his attention away from Rem like he was beneath regard and no competition.

Son-of-a-bitch.

Harry wanted Cara to himself.

"Cara!"

She turned back, juggling three leashes. "What?"

Rem pointed to the mutt. "He did that on purpose! He's mad because you gave him to me. He wants you for himself."

She gave him a pitying look. "Sure, Rem. I'm positive Harry has this big master plan to make your life torturous just because he wants to own me himself."

Oh, shit.

He sounded ridiculous. Still, one more glance at the mutt told Rem all he needed to know. The dog had a plan, alright, and Rem needed to keep an eye on him. "Come on, Harry," he said nicely. He'd try. For Cara's sake. After all, the dog didn't have a forever home. "Let's take a nice walk in the woods."

The dog looped his way around Rem's legs a few times, then tried to yank him off his feet.

Rem stumbled, tripped, and managed to avoid the tangle to keep the leash in his hold. Harry opened his mouth in an evident doggy sneer.

"Okay, Harry. I've had enough of you. This trip is gonna be a one way ticket into the woods like Hansel and Gretel."

"Rem!"

Ah, shit.

Cara's eyes widened with horror. Harry saw his opportunity and went into a crouch, whining pitifully like he'd been abused. "Here." She thrust the white French poodle's leash into his hand and grabbed Harry's. "Maybe you're not a good fit for him. He's had a hard life and needs a gentle hand."

Harry gave a nice doggy sigh.

Yeah. This friends thing was a real blast.

Somehow, she'd convinced him to help her out at the local pet shelter for the annual dog walk. Though he pointed out walking a bunch of dogs in a hundred degree heat wasn't a fun, friendly thing to do, her dedication and passion for rescues won out over his grumpiness. Rem had forgotten how enthusiastic and positive she was with lost causes. It was another thing that had made him easily fall in love with her.

As Cara led him and a few others down the trail for the official rescue walk, Rem admitted the past few weeks had been nice. When Cara first approached him about being friends, he'd been leery. How did he switch from hot, dirty sex to a hands-off relationship? How could he be friends with a woman he'd once loved and felt betrayed by? But one look at her eager face made him want to try.

After all, he'd originally believed their one night together would cure him forever. Rem figured he'd put the past behind and finally move on.

Instead, their one night had the opposite effect. Her touch and taste was permanently imprinted on his mind and body. Her offer of friendship could be the answer. Maybe he could end up getting the best parts from her, and let go of the others. They'd always been so close in other ways besides the physical. If Rem opened himself up to the possibility, maybe friendship would be the best thing for both of them.

So far, things were going well. They went to the movies and munched out on popcorn,

Raisinets, Slurpees, and then got sick. Sometimes after work, she stopped by and they strolled the mall together, sipping Starbucks and getting lost in the bookstore. Last night, they ate at a dive bar with a great local metal band, and ended up rocking out till dawn. Today, he'd met her at ten am and she put him right to work.

Rem was impressed. The other volunteers looked to her as a leader, and she took on the role with grace and warmth, from how she spoke to the public, treated the dogs, and kept everyone moving and on task.

She was Cara, but better. She didn't hesitate or question herself endlessly anymore. She didn't look to him for answers, or guidance. This woman knew what had to be done and owned herself—every part. How many times had her body issues broken his heart? He'd try to tell her how beautiful she was but she never truly believed it.

Those years away, she'd found herself. Claimed her beauty. Owned her soul.

It was the sexiest thing he'd ever seen in his life.

Rem figured he wouldn't like not being in charge all the time. He was so focused on having a full-time sub who would take his lead on all issues, he never thought about being in a relationship with a woman who only submitted in the bedroom. With Cara, it was nice to have a partner. She held her own, on every level, and Rem didn't have to be on all the time. It was kind of nice.

Not that it mattered, of course.

They were just friends.

Damn. He really wished he didn't want to fuck his new friend so bad.

The French poodle—Lacey?—walked nicely on the leash and didn't give him any back talk. Rem followed the trail, enjoying the view of Cara's tight jeans and full ass swinging back and forth. The volunteers chattered, laughed, and hid beneath the sting of the sun by heading into a nest of trees and letting the dogs go crazy with a variety of scents. Cara kept up a steady dialogue of what the DogCrazy animal shelter did, how many rescues it took care of, and what fostering entailed. He enjoyed listening to her voice, the dancing lilt and infused warmth that was part of who she was.

Lacey tried to hook up with a variety of studs, but unfortunately they seemed more interested in the excitement of the walk. Rem held back a laugh. Trying to get some action and getting rejected must be tough for a canine.

Poor little bitch.

"Uh, oh. I don't even want to know what thought you just had."

Cara stared at him with pure suspicion. Somehow, he'd been daydreaming and didn't catch her dropping back to match his stride. "You probably don't want to know."

"Try me."

"Umm, dog sex."

"Yeah, I don't want to know."

He burst into laughter. The sun exploded rays in her hair and lit them to fire. She smelled like earth and wild flowers. He tamped down an urge to lean forward and take a big sniff of her skin. Friends probably didn't do stuff like that.

Harry shot him a look of disgust, pulling on his leash to make Cara go faster.

"Do you have a dog?" he asked.

"No. I foster sometimes to help out the shelter, but I haven't made the leap yet. It's a big responsibility so I want to be sure."

"Yeah, Rome has a dog named Bella. She's a golden lab. He's crazy about her."

"I'd love to see your brothers again," she commented, stopping as Harry stuffed his nose in a pile of dirt. "But they probably hate me. I wouldn't blame them."

"They don't hate you, Cara. When I told them we spent the night together, they said we'd both made mistakes. I think they're right."

She groaned. "Oh, God, you told them we slept together? Now I'm really embarrassed."

"Why? Rafe was the one who hooked me up with FANTA-C. They all met their mates there."

"All of them? Wow, that's some serious juju."

She settled into quiet, and Remington spotted the faraway look she usually got when she was trapped in a memory. His heart ached, and he fought the urge to reach out and take her in his arms. Cuddle her close. How was it being with Cara soothed that restlessness that constantly haunted him?

No, he had to be careful. They both needed boundaries.

Maybe he'd go the club Chains tonight. It had been a long time between visits, but if he could find a sexy sub to entertain him and take his mind off fucking Cara, he may find some peace.

They finished the walk, and everyone gathered for a barbecue. He munched on hot dogs and hamburgers, helping at the grill, and distributing flyers to the crowd. Lacey hung by his side, chilled out, not needing a man to complete her.

As the day wound down, Cara trudged over with Harry cuddled in her arms. His chin rested on the generous curve of her breast. His gaze narrowed at Rem as they moved closer.

"Ready to wrap up and head home?" he asked. "I have an early shift in the morning."

His heart stuttered as she treated him to a full-blown smile with blinding white teeth. He almost stumbled back under the sheer power of feminine energy packing a punch. "I'm ready. So is Harry."

He cocked his head. "Huh?"

"That's the news! I'm adopting Harry! He's coming home with me."

Ah, shit.

Chapter Ten

"**Y**OU WERE WITH CARA AGAIN? Walking dogs?" Rick asked.

Rem shrugged and put up his hand to the cocktail waitress. His draft was quickly re-filled, and he faced his brother, Rick, who had a very nice handful sitting in his lap. Namely Tara Denton, the love of his life. Her silvery blonde hair made her look like an angel, and Rem believed she was damn close. "It was for the rescue shelter. She kind of convinced me to be a volunteer."

Rafe spit out a laugh. "Dude, you've never walked dogs for anyone else but her. So, what's the deal? It's been a few weeks and you always seem to be making plans with her. You two hooked up again?"

Rem glared. His other brother had his arms wrapped firmly around his current lover, Summer Preston. With her high ponytail, innocent face, and girl-next-door looks, no one would ever expect she was a wicked Dominatrix who'd beaten his brother and loved him like no other. Rem respected the hell out of her. She led the life she wanted, and finally convinced his brother to do the same. As former military, Rafe had been intent on ignoring his submissive side, afraid his family wouldn't understand.

Stupid. Rem respected the beauty of domination and submission on both sides, and it didn't matter whether the role was male or female. At least, Rafe had finally learned to embrace his real self.

Rem happened to love them already like sisters, so he hoped his brothers ended up making it official.

The ladies leaned forward. "Rem, is this the woman you dated through college?" Tara asked.

"That's the one."

"The one who stomped on your heart and left you for dead?" Summer asked with a protective frown.

He laughed. "Not really. Rafe has to do a better job explaining the intimate details of my past. Nothing like your brothers spilling your dirty laundry."

Tara waved her hand in the air. "We'd never share your secrets. It's in the circle of trust."

Rick tugged her hair playfully. "Hmm, seems you've been watching too many movies and not enough studying."

"I got an A- on my last test!"

"It should've been an A."

Rafe rolled his eyes. "Yeah, like you're a perfectionist, Rick. I saw your station before. It was a bit of a mess. Pop would've kicked your ass."

Tara giggled.

Rem figured this was a perfect time for his announcement. "Cara and I are friends now. I invited her to join us for a drink tonight."

Silence fell at the table.

"Friends?" Rick repeated. "Are you kidding me?"

"You're not sleeping with her?" Rafe asked in confusion.

"Nope. We're just friends."

"Who's friends?" Rem groaned at the sound of Rome's voice. Sloane greeted everyone and slid into the leather booth with a glass of sparkling water. Her dark good looks, and no-nonsense attitude screened a brilliant mind. As "The Queen of Cards" she made millions on the circuit and had just got back from another tour.

"Cara and Rem are now friends," Rafe filled in.

"Not the Cara who broke your heart and abandoned you?" Sloane asked.

"Is there anyone at this table that doesn't know my personal shit?" he grumbled.

"No," Rome said.

"Dude, you're screwed up," Rick said. "First you said you'd never see her again after the FANTA-C date. Now you're suddenly sneaking around, walking dogs, as *friends*. Why don't you both try again? It's obvious you're into her."

Rem glared and jabbed his finger at his brothers. "Stay out of this. "

Summer spoke up. "Rem is right, it's none of our business."

"I agree," Sloane said. "Hey, maybe you can take her to Chains?"

Rem choked on his beer. "No way. I know she had Paul teach her, but I'm sure she's ready to pull out of the club scene. I think we both needed FANTA-C to close the door on the past, and start fresh. But not together."

Silence fell again.

As he glanced around the table, he received sympathetic stares that told him one thing. He was a big chump.

"Well, this is a quiet table."

He looked up. Cara stood next to him, shifting her weight from foot to foot in her trademark gesture of nerves. Rem stood and gave her a half-hearted hug, feeling on display as the crowd in the booth took everything in. Sometimes, family was a real pain in the ass.

"I'm glad you can make it." He quickly made introductions to the girls, but his brothers surprised him. They slid out of the booth and caught up Cara in big bear hugs.

"You look great," Rick said. "All grown up."

Cara laughed and blushed. "You guys, too. I cannot believe I've been in Vegas over a year and never ran into you!"

Rome motioned to Rick. "Started with this guy, and one by one, he dragged us out here. Whatcha drinking?"

"Blue Moon on draft," Rem and Cara said together.

Rafe grinned. "Squeeze in with us."

She sat down and her leg pressed against his. He loved when she dressed up, but in a casual denim skirt, cowboy boots, and a white lace top, Cara Winters was drool worthy.

"How's Harry?" he asked grudgingly.

She smiled. "He's doing great. He'd been at the shelter a long time, and I was afraid he'd lost hope. He's literally the sweetest dog on the planet and now he's all mine."

The ladies sighed. Yeah, if they only knew Rem's days were numbered with the serial killer dog. "What do you do, Cara?" Sloane asked.

"I teach special education at Sommerset. I really love working with the kids."

Summer nodded. "I teach second grade at Lakeside. I swear, as tired as I get, those kids make it worth it."

The women bonded, chattering nonstop and slipping into girlie subjects that Rem wanted no part of. He relaxed in the booth, drank his beer, hung with his brothers, and enjoyed being next to Cara. The heat from her bare leg practically seethed through his jeans and burned him. The scent of musk drifted from her skin. So familiar. So enticing.

Like arousal.

The thought skittered past his brain and stopped. His dick was so hard, it strained his pants and made sitting so close uncomfortable as hell. Was she hot for him? If he slipped his hand underneath her denim skirt and between her thighs, would he find her wet for him?

"I heard Paul is treating you well over at Chains," Rick mentioned. "I'm glad. He's a good guy."

Cara didn't seem too nervous that Rick knew details. Since they were all involved in the lifestyle, no one had to worry about freaking out anyone else, and they talked as openly as they would in a club. Rem always told her it was hard to keep secrets from his brothers. It would drive most women batshit crazy, but Cara loved being involved in a large, noisy family. It was another part of her he adored so much.

"Yes. He thinks I'm ready to take on a public scene."

WTF?

His fingers jerked around his beer. "What are you talking about?" he demanded.

She looked at him, startled. "Paul thinks I'm ready to push myself a bit more."

"That's fucking ridiculous," he grated out. He fought back the simmering anger ready to explode. What was going on? He'd assumed Cara was backing out of the club after their night together. She wasn't ready for another Dom. Sure he'd wanted to tear Paul apart piece by piece for having his hands on her, but Paul was doing right by Cara allowing her to explore the BDSM world the right way. Still, she wasn't ready to display herself to a crowd who watched her. "A public scene is a big commitment. If Paul is pushing you, there's something seriously wrong."

Her gaze narrowed. Annoyance gleamed from meadow green eyes. "It's not Paul's decision, just his recommendation. I know if I'm ready or not, Rem," she said coolly. "But that's up to me. Not you."

"It certainly is up to me," he shot back. "You're not ready for that shit and I'm not letting you do it."

"You don't have a choice. You have no right."

"Watch me."

"No, Rem. You're my friend, remember. You don't want any more than that." Her voice dropped to a whisper. "You can't be both."

Her last words struck him like a meaty punch in the stomach. They stared at each other, the sexual energy whirling around them like a violent tornado. Rem smothered a violent curse, shaking with frustration.

Summer finally spoke up. "It's definitely a leap, but you'll know if you're ready. I did." Rafe took her hand and pressed her palm to his lips. "If this is a part of who you are, who you need to be, Chains is a good place to find it."

"Thanks." She forced a smile and stood up. "I have to go. Harry is still nervous when I leave him alone for too long."

"I'll walk you out," he said gruffly.

"No." The word lashed him like a whip. "I've got this. Thanks for letting me join you guys, tonight. I loved meeting everyone."

They said their goodbyes while Rem remained quiet. She walked away, and he stared at the table, taking note of the trickle of water linking his beer glass to hers.

"Rem?"

He looked up. Rick seemed to be the one to speak for all of them. "Go after her. Tell her you'll be her Dom at Chains. You belong together."

He'd thought that once before. He'd been wrong. He'd spent years questioning every move, every action, until he lay awake at night with a burning emptiness in his gut. His life after Cara had been a mess of jagged pieces he was desperate to put back into a puzzle. Now, she'd returned, and he wanted her just as bad. Logically, he understood he was still afraid of getting hurt. Afraid of not giving her what she needed. Afraid of failing them both.

"I can't," he said shortly. "It's better this way."

Frustration glimmered in Rick's eyes but he nodded his head. "Okay. We got your back, brother."

Sloane cleared her throat and raised her hand. "We'll need another round here."

Rem gave a grim smile and leaned back in the booth.

Chapter Eleven

CARA CHECKED IN AT THE FRONT desk of Chains and waited for Paul. Usually the club was filled with pounding music, orgasmic groans, the slap of whips and floggers, and the smell of sex. Since it was a weeknight and the club didn't open till nine pm, the place was quiet.

She had officially completed her lessons with Paul and they'd scheduled an exit interview. This was the time she could become a full member of the club, and he'd guide her into the first public scene.

Rem's reaction to the news confirmed he still held real feelings for her. Temper and possession had carved out the lines of his face; blasted from the heat of his gaze. She hadn't told him as a threat. She intended to fight for Rem as long as it took, but she had to show him she was her own person. He was no longer responsible for her happiness all the time. Cara had seen many

Dom/sub relationships and they worked in a variety of ways. In some, Doms took their submissive's contentment and day to day happiness as a sign of whether or not they're doing their job. For Cara, she already knew what she needed. A man to let her have a bad day, but comfort her. A man to strip her, beat her, pleasure her, and free her in the bedroom. A man who respected her, but didn't think every decision in her life was dependent on him.

She wanted a full blown partner. For life.

Cara was able to slay her own dragons, but damned if she didn't want a man to kick a little ass beside her, then kiss her wounds afterward to make them better.

"Cara?"

She smiled and hugged Paul. A big meaty man, with bulging muscles and a stout figure, his shaved head gave him a bit of a brutal look but was tempered by his beautiful brown eyes. She once told him they reminded her of a doe's and he threatened to beat her.

"Ready?"

"Yep."

"Follow me." He led her through the club and into the private offices toward the back. She sat on the red leather couch while he propped himself on the edge of the desk.

"You've come a long way, Cara." He crossed his arms in front of his chest and studied her. "I feel like you've grown a lot. Embraced the lifestyle. How do you feel about doing a structured, public scene?"

She raised her chin. "I want to do it."

"Let's go over limits, and expectations of the scene. I can be in charge, or set you up with one of the other Masters at the club."

"You, please."

"That's fine. You're also free to play with the other members. I can introduce you around on Saturday night to a few Doms."

She squirmed on the bench. There was one thing she learned about the lifestyle, and that was the need for honesty at all times. "Paul, there's only one man I'm interested in. He's already a member here. His name is Remington Steele."

He raised his brow in surprise. "Rem? Yeah, he's a regular. All of his brothers are members. Wait a minute, you're involved with Rem?"

"I spent one night with him. And we were involved when we were young. Now we're...friends."

He stared at her. "Friends, huh? With benefits?"

She gave a wobbly smile. "I'm still in love with him. I ran away years ago, afraid to tell him I was scared, and now I'm looking for a second chance."

Paul winced. "Communication is key in a relationship."

"I know. I was young and stupid. But I'm ready now, and know I can give him what we both need. I'm playing for keeps."

Paul shook his head. "Cara, this sounds like an emotional mess. Do you want me to talk to him? See where his head is at? Do you think he wants to do the scene with you?"

She dragged in a breath. "I think so. But he's holding himself back, because he's afraid he'll get hurt. I don't blame him. I'd like to push him so he realizes what's at stake for us."

"And you're using me to do it? Hell, if Rem considers you his, he'll tear apart any man in the way. Gonna put me in that position?"

"No, of course not. He knows you're my teacher and that we haven't been intimate. I told him everything. If I do this scene, maybe it'll give him a chance to—a chance to—"

"To what?"

She swallowed past the lump in her throat. "To claim me."

His face softened and he crossed the room, pulling her against him in a warm hug. "I'm sorry, baby girl. I have to warn you that it may not turn out how you want. He may choose to walk away if he sees you going into a scene. He may realize he can never really trust you again. Can you deal with that?"

She nodded against his chest. "I'm not giving up. But maybe this will tell me if I'm fighting for nothing. Maybe he'll never be ready to forgive me."

"You're playing a dangerous game, Cara. But I've also seen you grow through this practice. Come into yourself. You're beautiful when you submit, and it's a part of who you are. I think doing a public scene will help solidify that within you."

"Me, too."

"Then we'll do it together. And hope Mr. Steele doesn't kick the shit out of me."

***

Rem looked at his watch. He'd texted Cara hours ago and no response. His call went to voicemail. It was Saturday night and he was supposed to go to Chains. Find a submissive to play with and wring out some sexual frustration. There was just one problem.

He only wanted Cara Winters.

Since she'd mentioned doing a public scene at the club, Rem hadn't been able to stop thinking about it. About her submitting to another man. Letting him touch her. Bring her to orgasm. Scream his name and shatter apart.

The image taunted him every night, keeping him from sleep. No matter how many times he went over the rationale of remaining friends and keeping the past behind them, his heart smashed through the barriers and screamed for him to make a stand.

Cara was right all along. He had to eventually choose. Keep her as a friend and let her go? Break off their relationship completely and try again to banish her ghost? Or claim her for his once and for all?

But was he ready?

Seems like everything else didn't matter if he had an opportunity to see her. He dropped plans with his brother, rescheduled appointments, and tried to keep some shifts open in the evenings so he could sneak in a visit. When had it happened? When had seeing Cara become more important than anything else in his life?

His cell phone jumped and he quickly punched the button. His shoulders slumped at the sound of his brother's voice. "Hey, Rick. What's up?"

The line hummed. "You going to Chains tonight?"

He hesitated. Since he'd spent the night with Cara, Rem hadn't been to Chains to play. Sure, he'd gone in, talked to his friends, instructed some younger Doms on techniques of a scene, but he couldn't think of anyone else but Cara. "Nah, I'm in for the night. Why?"

Rick cleared his throat. "Look, dude, don't freak out. Especially if you're just *friends*. But Paul called me and said he's doing a public scene with Cara tonight at the club."

A roaring sound echoed in his ears. His blood thickened in his veins. "What did you say?"

"Cara's doing a scene. Look, bro, I have to say this or I'll regret it. She loves you. I saw it clearly at dinner—it's all over her damn face when she looks at you. If you still have feelings for her, let her know. Claim her tonight as your submissive. Life's too damn short for regrets or fear. Got it?"

"I gotta go."

The idea of another man's hands on her caused a primal rage to beat in his body. Private lessons with Paul was one thing. A public scene where a crowd watched his woman get naked and pleasured by some other Dom was not going to happen. Not with the woman he loved.

He had to get over there. Now.

Rem grabbed his phone and wallet, driving over to Chains in record time. He put his hand up in a brief greeting as he raced past Liliana at the front desk. The club was packed. The raw, throbbing music hit his ears as hard as the scent of leather and sex hit his nostrils. Rem made his way past the large dance area where writhing couples twisted and turned in a parody of sex. The lounge was a comfortable, open space with leather lounges and chairs, and erotic paintings hung on the red walls. He stopped at the crowded bar and motioned over to Easton, the bartender.

"Where's Paul?"

Easton jerked his head toward the private rooms. "Prepping for a scene." Easton was a perfectionist with a drink, knew who everyone was and where they were, and one of most popular Doms at Chains. He wore jeans, a cut off tank that emphasized roped arms, and his dirty blonde hair was tied back. He rarely dressed the part, preferring to filter his methods of control in ways other than clothes. "You okay, man? You look stressed."

"Nothing a good fight won't cure," Rem muttered under his breath. "Thanks."

He tore past the corridor, where various erotic scenes played out behind glass, and checked the Royalty room where Paul preferred to prepare, flinging open the door.

"What the hell—Rem?"

His fingers clenched. His nostrils flared with hot anger, and he shut the door behind him, grabbing for control. "Where is Cara?" he asked in a low voice.

Paul flinched, but he kept calm. "She's getting ready in the women's locker room. Summer is with her."

"Summer?"

"Rafe's Mistress."

"I know who Summer is, I'm just confused why she's in there with Cara helping her prep for a scene that's not going to happen."

Paul tightened his lips. "Calm down, Rem. Listen, Cara told me what was going on between the two of you, but she's trained for this and wants to do her first public scene. As a member here and Dom, you're welcome to step in and do the scene with her. Is that what you want?"

"She's not ready for this! Shit, I think she's only pushing herself to prove something to me."

"Maybe she just wants to prove it to herself," Paul said mildly.

"She doesn't know what she wants."

"I think she knows exactly what she wants. And so do you."

"Fuck you!"

"No thanks." Paul's delighted grin made him want to pounce and rage, but Rem knew the man was only trying to get him to admit the truth. The truth he'd known from that very first night she walked back into his life. "She's under my protection. I'm responsible for her well-being and she will be doing this scene. With or without you."

He strode over and got in Paul's face. Dropped his voice to a growl. "Cara is no longer under your protection. Get it? She's mine. She belongs to me, and I will be the one doing this scene with her."

Rem had to hand it to the Dom. Paul pushed him right to the edge. "Why? Convince me you're able to handle her better than I can."

"I love her, asshole!"

Paul grinned wider. "About damn time. She's set up for room 3. It's a sensation play scene—all the instruments are ready and on the table. She's got ten minutes. Need anything else?"

Rem pulled his shit together and turned his back. "No. I'll beat the crap out of you later."

Rem slammed the door on Paul's echoing laughter.

He weaved his way through various couples, nodding to a few, and reached the women's locker room. The truth shimmered in front of him. In a way, these last few years without her had been necessary. She'd learned to spread her wings and fly alone. And he'd learned not everything was always under his control, and love was bigger than past pain.

They'd both grown stronger apart, but together they were unbreakable.

It was time to claim her.

He knocked, and Summer peeked her head out. "Hi, Rem. I won't let you break down the door. Are you finally ready to admit she's more than a friend?"

He narrowed his gaze in warning. "You're just as meddlesome as my brother. Just because you wear black leather and hold a whip doesn't mean I can't take you on."

Her red lips widened into a smile. "Try me."

"I need to talk to her."

"Fine. You can come in and I'll stand guard." She strut out in a cat suit with a nasty looking flogger. "You have five minutes."

"You just met her. Why are you so protective?"

Summer winked. "You love her. Now she belongs to us."

A strange shivered bumped down his spine. He pushed inside and locked the door behind him.

"Rem?"

His eyes widened. Words jolted in his head, but none seemed able to come from his lips. She was—simply—breathtaking.

From her bright red hair framing her beautiful face, to her green eyes softly glowing as she looked at him, Cara was a Dominant's dream come true. The black lace top barely covered her straining breasts, and the tiny band of lycra stretched tight over her full curves, presenting her like a delicious present. Her feet were bare.

But it was the naked look of vulnerability that jolted him to the soul.

She loved him. It was carved out in the lines of her face, the longing in her eyes. It beat from every pore of her body, and the connection that always hummed between them surged to life, and exploded. It was time he show her just how much he loved her back.

"You don't have to do this scene," he said. "You already proved yourself. I don't need you to do a public display you're not ready for just to show me you can. You already submit to me completely, Cara. Do you understand?"

Her lower lip trembled. "I want to do the scene. I love this lifestyle, Rem. And I want it with you, more than anything. If you can ever forgive me."

He took a step forward. "I do. I understand so much more now, sometimes I have a hard time forgiving myself."

She shook her head hard, and the silky strands danced in the air, then settled against her cheeks. "No. If we do this, we start fresh. We're never going to be the people we were before, and I don't want that."

"What do you want? Because I sure as hell am done being just your friend."

Cara smiled at him. Her eyes shone with the wetness of tears. "You. Me. Us. Everything you have to give. Everything I can give."

"So do I." Rem took a step back, finally realizing what he needed to do. For both of them. The idea presented itself so clearly, an opportunity to move forward with a new trust. He dropped his voice to a strong, deep pitch. "I'd like to scene with you, Cara. From now on, there will never be another man allowed to touch you, instructor or not. Understood?"

She shook, and her pupils dilated. Good. She knew they were about to move into scening, and the rules now applied. Her body peaked, ready to play. Rem knew the simple traditions of speaking in a different voice was like the flick of a switch.

Cara was fully lit up, and ready to follow him.

"Yes, Sir."

"Very good. You will come with me to the stage, and I will present you to the audience. Tell me about the scene Paul prepared you for?"

"Sensation play, Sir. I'm to lie on the table while he demonstrates how various instruments causes pain or pleasure."

"And were you allowed to orgasm?"

"Yes, Sir."

What is your safeword?"

"Red."

"If you begin to panic, you say the word yellow and I'll slow down. Are you ready, Cara?"

"Yes, Sir."

"Give me your hands"

Rem would normally chain her wrist and guide her to the stage, but he hadn't prepared. Instead, he bound her by his will and command, which was even more powerful. His fingers wrapped firmly around her delicate wrist.

"Follow me. Head down. Let's begin."

"Yes, Sir."

Rem led her out, nodding to Summer as they passed the crowds waiting for the public scene to begin. He walked into Room 3. The room was equipped with a padded table, a couch, blankets, bottles of water, and an open cabinet full of interesting equipment guaranteed to get his woman off.

He couldn't wait.

The heavy weight of the stares from the crowd only jacked up the arousal and anticipation of what was to come. Cara trembled, and he pulled her to him, lifting her chin up so she was forced to face him.

"I intend to worship you, Cara. Give you pleasure. Make you come. Prove you've always been mine."

He swallowed her sweet gasp with his mouth over hers. Plunging his tongue between her lips, he drank up her essence and taste, drowned in sweetness, and came back whole. When he pulled away, she looked back with dazed eyes, and he slowly released her and took a step back.

"Present yourself."

With graceful motions, she pulled the tiny lace top over her head, folded it neatly, and lay it down. Her bare breasts hung heavy and ripe. Red nipples begged for his tongue and teeth, already hard and swollen with need. She stepped out of her skirt, placed it on top of the shirt, and knelt before him. Legs widespread, arms clasped behind her, she humbled herself before him with dignity and a searing beauty that branded him for life.

"You are beautiful. Do you know that?"

"I am if you think so, Sir."

"I know so. I also know everyone is watching you and wanting you. But you belong to me, don't you Cara?"

"Yes, Sir."

He moved around her, stroking her hair, tweaking a nipple. His hands ran down her spine, catching her shiver, and slid between her legs. Dripping heat met his strokes, and he held back a groan at her readiness. God, she was perfect. Ripe for fucking and taking what's his. Ripe for only him.

"Gorgeous." He held up his hand and licked his fingers. "My sub is ready. Please lie on the table."

She rose to her feet and situated herself on the table. With a wicked smile, he slid out the two stirrups hidden in the table, and placed her feet on each of them so she was spread wide. Doctor play was popular, but he kept a close eye on her, wanting to be sure this was something that turned her on.

One more dip of his fingers into her cunt proved it did.

The table also had slide outs for her hands, so he quickly bound her wrists with the soft leather ties, and gazed upon the woman he loved.

Spread wide. Wet with arousal. Her clit was already hard, and poking from the hood. Nipples hard little points. She squirmed with need, obviously loving that they had a crowd watching her. Who would've thought his shy little Cara would have an exhibitionist streak? He loved discovering every naughty little thing about her, and intended to spend the rest of his life dedicated to acting out every one of her fantasies.

He hoped she had a lot of them.

"The rules are simple, Cara. No coming unless I give you permission. No moving. But you may scream as loud as you'd like." He turned toward the table of instruments. "Let's begin."

Chapter Twelve

*C*ARA SUNK DEEPER INTO a world of decadence and submission. The man she loved, from the moment his hungry gaze caught hers in English 101, was about to wreak havoc on her very willing body.

God, she couldn't wait.

The knowledge he loved her allowed her to let go and fly. This was a new start for both of them, and Cara was already wet and aching for him to thrust into her pussy and claim her.

But first he'd torture her.

"Do you see what I'm holding, Cara?"

She blinked and focused. He held a large white feather. Cara relaxed. "Yes, Sir."

"What is it?"

"A feather, Sir."

"Do you know what I can do with this feather?"

"Tickle me?"

A half smile kicked up his lips. "Many things. Let's see. I will not blindfold you, but I want you to close your eyes. Do not open them until I tell you. Understand?"

"Yes, Sir."

Her lids slid closed and she relaxed against the table. A light tickling sensation skated over her sensitive skin, bringing goose bumps. From her chin, down her sides, around her knee, ankle, to the tip of her toes, he teased her into a state of complete arousal, but it came with gentle waves instead of violent tsunamis. Ah, she could do this all day. Pure heaven. If only he—

The feather traced the line of her bare pussy, the crease between thigh, and slowly, touched the tip of her clit.

She jerked. Her eyes flew open.

His face was implacable, but a glint of amusement lit his ocean blue eyes. "You will not open your eyes, Cara, or you will be punished. Do you understand?"

"Yes, Sir."

"Your body is stunning. You were meant to be adorned with jewels. I'd choose rubies to go with your hair. Why don't we see how you'd look?"

She held her breath and heard rustling from the right side. Heart pounding madly, she waited for his touch. His fingers closed around her hard nipple, stroking. She let out a sigh, and then his hot mouth sucked on her, his tongue flicking and lapping at the tight bud until it was long and hard and so sensitive.

A pinch stabbed her nipple. Her tummy tightened and tumbled in a free-fall. God, it felt so strange. A good hurt. She heard the delicate tinkling of chains. "Gorgeous. Now the other one."

Cara wanted to open her eyes, but he hadn't given permission. He treated the other breast to the same, licking and sucking, making the tip long, and then another pinch clamped around her nipple.

"Stunning. Open your eyes, Cara. Look at yourself."

She obeyed. Tiny rubies hung from the nipple clamps and a gold chain loops both together. The tight, painful sensation softened, until her blood ran hot and thick, and arousal settled heavily between her thighs. Oh, God, she was so turned on, she needed desperately to come. She felt so sensitive, and needy. Rem tugged on the chain and a lightning streak of heat shot to her clit, wrestling a moan from her lips.

"Ah, you like that. I'm glad. You may close your eyes again, Cara."

She whimpered. Her muscles clenched as he began to play. The feather dipped inside her, tickled her clit, then slid up her stomach to torture her nipples. Flicking the tips back and forth, she moaned and forced herself not to shoot up and demand her orgasm. Who would've thought a damn feather could make her want to rocket off the table?

She had no idea where the next touch would land, and the not knowing made the waiting even more excruciating. Finally, the feather dipped into her navel, moved lower, and began to rotate around her clit. Again. Again. He tugged on the chain and her nipples flared to life.

Uh, oh.

Cara bore down and fought off the impending climax, but he was merciless. The gentle, steady manipulation was like a stream of a shower jet, and she panted, trying to maintain control.

At the last minute, when she was ready to beg, he backed off.

Thank God.

Until a hot searing burn raked across her nipple.

Cara arched under the sting. Pain, then pleasure exploded in waves. She was desperately trying to figure out what was happening, when the feather began the slow circling torture, and as her mind tried to cling to that sensation, another burning sting enveloped the tip of her other breast.

A candle? Hot wax? Oh, god, she wasn't going to make it.

The play continued. Blistering heat. Coolness as the wax hardened. A slow circle around her clit. A drag of the feather over her pussy. Again. And again.

Everything tensed up and drew tight, ready for release, but each time he brought her back from the edge and gave her a breather.

"Oh, please," she moaned, squeezing her eyes tight. She shook on the table, trying to maintain control. "Sir, I'm going to come."

"You will not."

Suddenly, a bitter cold object was pressed against her clit. Her hips jerked madly upward, and she screamed as an ice cube was slowly pushed into her hot, swollen pussy. The extreme mingling of hot with cold threw her into mini convulsions, and wiped out any lingering ideas her mind had of keeping stock on what was going on.

In that one moment, Cara surrendered.

Time merged into intervals of sensation, and she let her body rule and become her own master. She hung somewhere in space, filled with blinding colors and sharp pleasure; a place where her mind couldn't follow.

She didn't know how long he was whispering her name until she came to, and drowsily opened her eyes.

"My sweet, good girl. My beautiful, Cara. Do you want to come?"

"Yes."

"Beg me, Cara."

A sob choked her throat. "Please, Sir. I want you so much. I love you—please—"

She hissed out a breath when his warm, wet mouth closed over her clit, sucking gently, flicking the hard nub back and forth with his tongue. The orgasm built, driving her forward like a hurtling freight train, until she hung on the edge, desperate for release, her head thrashing back and forth.

"Come, Cara. Come for me, my love."

He ripped off the nipple clamps, and as searing pain hit her tortured nipples, he bit down on her clit, and she was coming.

Cara screamed and screamed, her body jerking under the violent spasms of lust and release, coming over and over. He held her tight to the table and sucked and licked her pussy, driving into her second orgasm. Finally, she collapsed, tears sliding down her cheeks, and gave herself over completely.

He released her from the bonds, picked her up, and wrapped her in a warm blanket. Leaving the crowd behind, he walked off stage and into a small private room and dropped into a chair, rocking her against his chest. "Drink, sweetheart."

Cara took a few sips. The water soothed her raw throat. Gazing up at him, she realized there was nowhere left to hide for either of them. And she gave him the words.

"I love you, Remington Steele. I want to be your submissive. Your lover. Your best friend. I want to be your everything. I will never leave you, and I beg you for one more thing." She trembled in his arms. "Love me as much as I love you. Give me another chance."

He muttered something under his breath and took her mouth in a deep, ravishing kiss. When he lifted his head, those blue eyes burned with a truth that wouldn't be hidden.

"You never have to beg me to love you, Cara. I always have, and I always will. I want to be your

Dom, your lover, your friend. I want to be your husband. And I'll never leave you."

Cara reached for him, caressing his cheeks, pressing her forehead to his. Her soul soared with the possibility of a new life with him, one where they didn't have to beg each other for anything at all.

One filled with love.

The End

Jennifer's Playlist

After All - Cher/Peter Cetera

All You Had to do was Stay - Taylor Swift

Damn I Wish I was Your Lover - Sophie Hawkins

Give It To Me - Justin Timberlake and Nelly
Furtado

I Bet My Life- Imagine Dragons

Insensitive - Jann ARden

Lie To Me - Rob Thomas

Please Don't Go - Mike Posner

Stitches - Shawn Mendes

Where'd You Go - Holly Brook & Jonah Matranga

Books by Jennifer Probst

THE STEELE BROTHERS SERIES
Catch Me
Play Me
Dare Me
Beg Me
Reveal Me

THE BILIONAIRE BUILDERS SERIES
Everywhere and Every Way
Any Time, Any Place
All or Nothing at All

SEARCHING FOR SERIES
Searching for Someday
Searching for Perfect
Searching for Beautiful
Searching for Always
Searching for Disaster

MARRIAGE TO A BILLIONAIRE
The Marriage Bargain
The Marriage Trap
The Marriage Mistake
The Marriage Merger

1001 DARK NIGHTS
Somehow, Some Way: A Billionaire Builders Novella
Searching for Mine: A Searching For Novella

About the Author

Jennifer Probst is the New York Times, USA Today, and Wall Street Journal bestselling author of both sexy and erotic contemporary romance. She was thrilled her novel, The Marriage Bargain, was the #6 Bestselling Book on Amazon for 2012. Her first children's book, Buffy and the Carrot, was co-written with her 12 year old niece, and her short story, "A Life Worth Living" chronicles the life of a shelter dog. She makes her home in New York with her sons, husband, two rescue dogs, and a house that never seems to be clean. She loves hearing from all readers! Stop by her website at http://www.jenniferprobst.com for all her upcoming releases, news and street team information.